Claiming Christmas

Alex & Alexander: Book Four

Natalie Keller Reinert

Natalie Keller Reinert Books

Chapter One

THE PHONE WAS RINGING and I wasn't answering it.

I'd stopped answering my phone two weeks ago and honestly, I couldn't have been happier with my decision. It had been a long hot summer, even if I had spent it in Saratoga and not in Florida, and now I just needed to *relax*. No more people crowding me, whether in the barn or on the phone.

And it was wonderful, this hermit life. No more owners with pie-in-the-sky requests and questions they could have figured out for themselves if they had spent thirty seconds in the company of Google. No more supplement salesmen trying to pitch me the latest and greatest in equine supplement breakthroughs "that test clean, we guarantee!"

No more little kids calling to ask how much riding lessons were.

That one was always particularly annoying, although, if I was perfectly honest with myself, I could remember running my finger down the listings of stables in the Yellow Pages, calling each and every likely-sounding business name in the category, asking that very question with the same tremulous voice.

However, chances were that today's kids had access to a decent search engine which could have told her which stables taught riding lessons versus which stables taught horses to run very quickly in circles.

So I didn't feel as guilty as I might have when I replied, every single time one of them called: "Listen, kid, we don't teach—this is a *racing* stable, okay?"

No, I *wasn't* mean when I said it.

I was just *brisk*.

But I wasn't dealing with *any* of those annoyances anymore. I was making a clean break from technology. Well—not quite. I was still using my phone for practical matters, like checking the weather radar, and scrolling through Twitter for racing news. I was on top of things now, baby. When thunder started rumbling before an afternoon thunderstorm, I was already strolling back to the house, the horses in their stalls and the barn doors closed. When a big-shot trainer did something stupid or some top-of-the-line three-year-old colt was suddenly retired to stud "completely sound" I was the first to read the press release and come to my own (skeptical) conclusions. I enjoyed knowing the weather, and I enjoyed knowing everything about racing before Alexander, so in this regard, my phone had really become indispensable to me.

But I wasn't answering it for anyone. I just wasn't up to talking to people at the moment. Call it a phase.

I talked to the horses, though. It was a very peaceful sort of conversation, my horse-human dialogues. I spoke, and they blinked, or sighed, or snorted, or did nothing at all, and it was perfect.

And I talked to Alexander, although at this very moment I strongly suspected I didn't want to do that—just a guess, judging the current stormy expression on his face.

Alexander was glaring at me from across the kitchen with the sort of half-disappointed, half-exasperated expression he reserved especially for me and badly behaving older horses. As if we—myself and the older horses—should both know better, but were *choosing* to be bad *solely* to put him out. It wasn't true well, it might have been true of the horses, but it wasn't true of me—but he was certainly entitled to his opinion. Especially since he got the short end of the stick anytime I did misbehave in the eyes of the racing community. If I was playing the hermit, that meant Alexander had to pick up the slack. And neither of us were precisely social butterflies by nature.

Even so, Alexander was the good one, as usual, and he picked up the ringing phone, eyeballing me all the while with a gaze which promised a Talk was coming. "Cotswold Farm," he said in a mannerly tone, despite the fact that it was our house number and it was seven thirty in the evening. Every hour was business hours with Alexander.

I went into the living room and turned on The Weather Channel.

I was just getting deeply invested with some extensive coverage of a weather system impacting the Northern Plains with high winds and a mixture of rain and snow when Alexander came into the room.

I didn't look away from the television. "It's going to snow like hell in Chicago," I predicted happily. "In *October*. Who lives like that? Don't you have a friend up there now?"

"He moved," Alexander said, sitting on the sofa next to me. He leaned on the sofa arm, away from me, and rested his head on his hand, flicking his eyes disinterestedly towards the television. "To Barbados."

"Smart move." I went on watching the meteorologist describe the falling barometric pressure at the center of the storm, located approximately ten miles from Nowhere, North Dakota. "How do they *know* the barometer is falling? There's nothing out there."

"Satellites," he said absently. "Weather nuts living on farms."

I looked over at him then, finally noticing he wasn't fully present. "Who was on the phone?" I asked, suddenly concerned.

"Linda."

"Linda who?" There were about forty-seven Lindas in the Ocala Thoroughbred community. Some were wives of prominent breeders and owners; some were sport or show-horse trainers; one owned Linda's Tackeria and Feed Store in Lowell. I liked the Tackeria and Feed Store Linda best of all: she was about fifty years old, had platinum blond hair, and wore denim jackets adorned with air-brushed western scenes of cacti and sunsets. No pearls or polyester pant-suits for that Linda. She was *all* about the desert and needed to share this passion every day. The fact that her accent was pure Appalachia made her that much better, in my opinion. But there was no chance that was the Linda he was talking about—I was fairly certain she didn't even know my name, let alone have any reason to call us at seven thirty at night. We didn't have an account at the Tackeria; it was just a place I dropped by from time to time, to admire her jacket du jour.

Alexander shifted on the couch, reached beneath him, and pulled a dee-ring bit from under the cushion. "What the hell?"

I took it from him, only a little embarrassed. I had been wondering what became of that bit for a week and a half. "Which Linda, seriously? There's like a million."

"Linda Swanson," Alexander clarified, eyeing the bit in my hand. "From Stonewood Stables. Are you going to explain the bit, Alex?"

"No." There really wasn't anything to explain; it had been in my jacket pocket from a quick bridle change the other morning and I must have pulled it out and forgotten about it while I was watching TV. But I enjoyed knowing he was now trying to guess scenarios which involved a bit and the living room sofa. Brainteasers were good for Alexander. They kept him young. "Are you going to explain why Linda Swanson is calling you late at night?"

He sighed and flung his head back. "It's not even eight o'clock at night."

"She's old. She goes to bed early." Linda Swanson was probably all of sixty, but her coral lipstick and teased mass of cropped white hair did not do her any favors.

Alexander ignored my nonsense; he was good at that. "She called on behalf of the Rodeo Queens."

"The *Queens?* Oh God, what do they want?" The Rodeo Queens were a clique of wealthy racehorse widows who had designated themselves the premier do-gooders in town. We weren't short of equestrian-related philanthropy in this town, but the Rodeo Queens were a breed apart, as tightly knit as their twin-sets and apparently about as knowledgeable of horses as they were about the dangers of tanning oil. Just their name alone, Rodeo Queens, made absolutely no sense. Not a single one of them had anything to do with rodeos. Their husbands all made their money in racehorses. It made me crazy. "Their name makes zero sense, do you realize that? Do they even know what a rodeo *is?*"

Alexander waited for me to finish.

I subsided. "How can we help the fine ladies of the Rodeo Queens tonight? Do they want to have a fundraiser here? Because they can't."

"Why would they want to have a fundraiser here? Don't be silly. This house is like a nightmare to them. Too minimalist.

Plus no one would ever believe you could hostess a party. No, it's something else...it's interesting. It's like a wish-granting situation. They grant a Christmas wish every year. There's a little girl who has had a rough time of things, and they picked up her case, and it turns out her wish is to go to the races with you and see Personal Best run a race."

I was so astonished, I couldn't think of anything snarky to say. I just turned and stared at Alexander. He looked back at me with a faint expression of triumph, as if he'd been waiting for my dumbfounded reaction.

"I can't understand it either," he chuckled after a few moments had passed. "Obviously this girl knows nothing of your disposition."

"I have a *lovely* disposition." I considered throwing a handy pillow, merrily embroidered with riding crops and spurs, at his smirking mug. "It is outdone only by my exquisite conformation."

"Your legs are too long," Alexander said dismissively. "You'll never stay sound."

I burst out laughing and threw the pillow at him anyway. He caught it and hugged it around his middle, grinning at me. "What's that about your temper? Anyway, listen to me—" and his face grew serious again—"Linda's coming over on Tuesday to have a chat with you about having this girl down to Gulfstream with you at the weekend."

I stopped laughing. We had Personal Best in the Loxahatchee Stakes next weekend. It was meant to be his last race as a two-year-old, before we brought him home and gave him some downtime for December and January. He had been in training pretty consistently ever since the Saratoga meet, and had brought home a win and a couple of near-misses. He hadn't made it to the Breeders' Cup, but there was always next year. I didn't feel like going all the way to California anyway. I was tired from our year of campaigning; I figured he was probably feeling that way, too.

Going to the races for the weekend was fun, but having some kid hanging around—I didn't like that idea one bit. Especially if it meant I had to deal with Linda or any other Rodeo Queen. "No way." I turned my attention back to The Weather Channel, where a handyman was demonstrating how to make a fitted window screen. "Since when do windows come without screens?"

"Not everywhere is Florida," Alexander reminded me. "In some places, you can open your windows and you won't even get dengue fever."

"I don't believe it."

"It's a big world." Alexander leaned his head back again and closed his eyes. "Alex—listen."

I stiffened.

"You have to stop this."

"Stop what?" He was being purposefully vague.

"Stop ignoring the phone, for starters."

"And for seconds?"

"Maybe start interacting with humans in the world again?"

I pretended to think about it. "No, I'm good, thanks."

"Alex."

"Alexander," I intoned dramatically, and gave his thigh a good-natured squeeze. "Humor me in this. I am taking a vacation from the world. Shouldn't everyone get one of those every now and then? I promise you can have one as soon as I get back."

"You're going to help Linda out with this," he said implacably.

"How am I going to drag some kid around at the track? I have work to do. This isn't like a beach weekend or something."

"You'll hardly be alone. And she'll be chaperoned. You're just going to show her around a bit and then give them someplace to stand out of the way." Alexander had on his I'm-the-One-Being-Reasonable face. It made me crazy. "I thought you'd be honored someone's big wish is to spend the day with you."

Hardly. "I thought everyone wished to go to Disney World."

"Not everyone, apparently."

"*I* would wish to go to Disney World."

"Well, you're you. It's only natural that you'd like to take a break from yourself for a day."

I lunged for the pillow, intent on giving him the beating he deserved, but Alexander managed to not only hang on to the pillow but get an arm around me in a bear hug, pulling me tight across his chest. I shrieked with laughter and threw myself forward and we both went tumbling off the sofa and onto the floor, where I managed to knock my head on the coffee table and saw stars, which kind of ended the hilarity for the night.

The fact was, we were just too old to wrestle on the floor like teenagers. So we took it upstairs, like the civilized adults that we were, and I forgot all about Linda the Rodeo Queen, and the anonymous girl whose Christmas wish was to visit me and my racehorse.

Chapter Two

KERRI THOUGHT IT WAS hilarious, of course. "Have you ever even talked to a kid? I've never seen you anywhere near one."

"I've talked to a kid," I snapped, which was pretty impressive because I had a mare's tail draped across my collarbone and over my shoulder. I spit a horse-hair out my mouth and resolved to keep my mouth shut while Dr. Dee had her arm inside the mare. But Kerri, nice and safe at the mare's head, thought baiting me in such a compromised state was pretty fabulous.

"Is it possible that you are actually child-repellant? I've never even seen a kid come *near* you. Like, even at Saratoga where there are kids basically everywhere, you have this bubble around you. Wow, Alex, seriously? Kids *hate* you. This might end really badly. Maybe you better say no."

"I can't say no," I said matter-of-factly. "It's for *Christmas.*"

"Do you even celebrate Christmas? I had you pegged for a hates-holidays type, as well."

"Of course I celebrate Christmas." But I didn't, not *really*. Aside from buying the grooms turkeys and sticking a few red bows on the farm gates, Christmas was another day on the farm. Horses still needed feeding and cleaning up and training. They still got hurt, they still kicked down fence-boards, they still ripped the piping out of pasture waterers and flooded the fields. It was hard to be passionate about a holiday with the workload that we had. "There just isn't much time to bother with it, is all."

"That and no kids to bother with."

"There's that." The mare yanked her tail, trying to get it out of my hands, and I took a firmer grip. "I have enough kids with all these horses, anyway."

"Something a crazy cat-lady would say," Kerri observed. "If they were cats."

"Are you calling me a crazy horse-lady?"

"Maybe I am. You're just going to get older and scarier and have more horses and the neighborhood kids will never get a ball that goes over your fence."

I gritted my teeth. The vet pulled her arm free of the mare with that tremendous wet sucking sound that never leaves your ears after the first time you hear it, and stripped off the lube-streaked glove. "All set."

"Thank God," I said, dropping the tail. "Kerri, you're on tail duty next time. I'm the boss and I'm done with this."

"You said *doody*!" Kerri howled from inside the stall, walking the mare back in and turning her to face the doorway.

"What are you, five years old? Shut up."

"I was just testing you to see if you could handle humor. Kids love the humor. Bad news, you failed." She came out of the stall and slid the door closed, wrapping up the lead-shank in her hands, and made a face at me, sticking out her tongue and crossing her eyes.

"Whatever," I said, because I am the queen of comebacks.

Dr. Dee stared. She was new to the team at our vet clinic and didn't know that we couldn't behave normally to save our lives. "It's Kerri's fault," I told her.

"It's Alex's fault, always," Kerri informed her gravely.

"Mare looks good," Dr. Dee said desperately. "I'll give you a call if we find anything."

She fled the barn.

Kerri grinned at me. I just shook my head.

"So tell me again," Kerri began, as we went rattling down the barn drive in the golf cart. "This is a Make-A-Wish thing?"

"No...I thought so too." When Linda had come over to discuss the kid who wanted to spend the day with me, she had explained that Wendy Ludwig had had a hard time of things— her parents had been killed in a car accident, and she was living with her grandmother in a single-wide trailer in Citra since she was little. But now her grandmother was having health problems too—Linda wasn't specific, and I didn't ask—and someone called the Rodeo Queens and asked them to take her on as their yearly Christmas Wish recipient. "She's just had a really rough life, orphaned and her grandmother's sick, and she loves horses but she can't have one, obviously, because there's no money...so apparently she told the Rodeo Queens that her Christmas Wish was to go to the races with me and see Personal Best."

"Seems like the Rodeo Queens got off cheap this year. Didn't they save a farm from foreclosure for the Christmas Wish last year?"

I laughed. Kerri was so wonderfully cynical these days. I was rubbing off on her, for better or for worse. Mainly worse. Being my assistant could only end badly for a person. "They're going to do something else for her. Riding lessons for a year, or for life, or something."

"That's more like it." Kerri turned the golf cart towards the training barn. It was quiet up there now, all the horses napping or working at their hay-nets. The grooms would be in their apartments napping or watching the races from the satellite feed. Two o'clock in a racing barn is a peaceful time. "You know I can't go with you, right? I have a breeding seminar all day."

I sighed. Kerri's formal education aspirations were taking her away from her valuable job of helping me do absolutely everything. "I'm not going to pay you more when you have an Equine Science degree, you know."

"I know it." Kerri pulled the golf cart up in front of the barn entrance. Several horses nickered a hopeful hello, evidently suspecting an early supper might be offered. "That's why I'm going to start my own business."

"You wouldn't. You can't live without me." I leaned my head back against the seat. "Grab the training book from the tack room, wouldja? I want to go over it with Alexander tonight."

Kerri cast me a withering look, which said all she wanted it to about my decision to be lazy in the golf cart while she did the rounds to check bandages, buckets, and hay nets. I closed my eyes in response. Baiting Kerri was better than ice cream.

⋙⋙ ⋘⋘

Linda called while we were going through the training log. Alexander took one look at me that meant business, so I got up and picked up the phone. "Hi Linda," I said warily. "How are things."

"ALEX!"

Oh, dear God. Enthusiasm was so tiring. "That's me."

"I have *news.*"

"Okay." I rolled my eyes at Alexander, who took a long sip of wine and smiled at me.

"Little Wendy is very excited! She is going to meet you on Saturday morning at the security gate. Her Aunt Karen is bringing her, but she doesn't know a thing about horses so you will have to be *vigilant!* And keep an eye on her! Her aunt might not know any better and let her get too close to a horse!"

So far, Linda was using far more exclamation points than I was comfortable with. She was also asking me to do the impossible. Baby-sit a kid *and* her aunt on a race day—on a *stakes* race day. Something told me she would never have asked her *husband's* racing trainer to do something so ludicrous. "Linda, you understand I have a horse in that day, right?"

There was a pause on the other end. I imagined Linda's carefully made up face collapsing into a frown of confusion, then realized that of course that wasn't possible, thanks to Botox. I settled for Linda looking blank, which was her normal expression when I was forced into stilted conversation with her, so actually that was much easier to picture. "Of course," she finally said, a hint of a stammer in her words. "But you did—we *agreed*—she is coming with you *to* the races, that was the entire request—"

"I know that. I'm just saying that I can't be the chaperone for a little kid here. I am a racehorse trainer, I am not a baby-sitter—" I paused to throw a wadded-up napkin at Alexander, who was chortling at my predicament—"And you're going to have to be sure whoever *is* the baby-sitter doesn't need me watching them every second of the day. They can show up and they can watch, but they have to stay out of my way and not bug me. Tell them that...nicely...will you please? I don't want them to think I'm some sort of tour guide. I'm a professional—"

"I understand you're a professional," Linda replied in a more steely tone.

"Well, good." I chewed my lip for a minute, trying to think of something else to say. Linda was helpfully silent. Alexander had given up teasing me and had gone back to the training ledger. I saw him frowning at a work-out time and decided I'd wasted enough time on Linda. "Tell them I'll see them Saturday," I finished. "Night, Linda. Appreciate all your hard work."

"Yes, thank you—" Linda was saying, but I hung up, ready to move on with my actual work.

"I see you questioning that time," I told Alexander. "Here's what happened..."

Chapter Three

I HAVE TO ADMIT, I obsessed a lot about the kid on the long drive to south Florida. Because Kerri was right—I wasn't a person kids liked. Or talked to. Or looked at without running away. I would never have told Kerri that all her teasing the other day had gotten under my skin—she would have felt terrible—but I had to admit, this one really worried me.

I thought kids could tell I didn't like them. Kids are like dogs, or horses—they still have all their natural instincts in place. They're still half-wild, feral creatures, trying to decide if they want to follow the rules or run away and live in the woods. They sense things that adults do not, because adults have given in to following the rules, and don't need those survival senses anymore. That's my theory, anyway, as half-baked as it might be. Some people attract children like magnets; I do not, and I have never really let that bother me. Horses are far more interesting, in my opinion. And you can leave them in the barn at the end of the work-day.

But this kid *wanted* to meet me. What was that about? Why on earth would anyone want to meet *me,* for starters, kid or not? Who was I? Just a horse trainer with a few wins, nothing special. I was used to being in Alexander's shadow, that much was true, but even then, Alexander was only horse-famous. No one outside of the racing world had a clue who he was, and very few people *in* the industry would have recognized him on the street, or even on the backside. Honestly, neither of us were exactly setting the world on fire with our horses. Personal Best was doing nicely, but my mare Luna was training like a dud in south Florida. She hadn't won a race since the Saratoga meet. The others were all holding their own at their levels, but I just didn't have a world-beating stable right now. And that was okay—not every season was a record-breaker—it just made this situation particularly strange.

Alexander wasn't much help; he found the whole thing equal parts amusing and bizarre. "I don't know, why *would* anyone want to meet you?" he teased when I asked him what he thought, and I nearly drove off the road when I reached across the sedan's interior to give him a well-deserved smack over the head.

"You're not helping," I told him, and he laughed.

"This is what you get," my beloved and devoted husband went on after he had laughed his fill. "Just think, if you hadn't been playing hooky from the telephone you could have picked it up and said no to Linda without my ever knowing a thing."

And that was when I knew *he'd* told Linda I'd escort the kid around the racetrack. Just to get back at me for my vacation from the world. "You're the worst," I told him.

"You love me."

I turned up the radio then. Because I did, but he didn't need to hear me say it to know it was true.

And anyway, I wouldn't have said no to a little girl's Christmas wish. Would I?

Personal Best had picked up this way of leaning out over his stall webbing to see me, his ears pricked and his eyes bright, bellowing out a welcoming whinny as if he had thought he'd never lay eyes on me again, and then retreating to the back of his stall and refusing to come and see me until I offered him a peppermint. It was not at all becoming of a great racehorse, who should be professional and workmanlike at all times, and it was also absolutely adorable.

I leaned over his webbing and crinkled a piece of plastic in my hand to let him know I had the mint he was waiting for, all the while admiring the hind end he was pointing in my direction. His big muscled quarters were defined and gleaming, and his red tail, which finally reached his fetlocks, was freshly brushed and shimmering with golden highlights.

"You're not a baby anymore," I told him. "Look at that long tail." He cocked an ear in my direction and turned to look at me. I held up the mint and he acquiesced with a sigh, walking to the webbing and digging his nose into my palm for the candy.

"Sweet boy," I told him, leaning my head against his for just a moment. Then he pulled back, abruptly, and regarded me with his soft brown eyes while he chomped at the treat. Mint breath spilled from his mouth as if he had just brushed his teeth. "Minty fresh," I said, and moved down the line to see Luna, who was waiting for me, leaning against her webbing, alert to the possibility of peppermints.

She took her mint more daintily, with a little wiggle of the upper lip to scoop the candy from my fingertips; Personal Best would have eaten my fingers if I tried to just hand him a treat like that. While she crunched down on the peppermint I admired her funny-face blaze, the big blob of chestnut smack in the middle of the white streak that ran from forelock to nose. "I love your silly face," I told her, and she snorted, blowing peppermint breath all over me.

I sighed with happiness, because these were my children, my two chestnut children, and I had missed them so much.

Alexander was talking to Brian, the trainer who was handling our horses while they were in south Florida. I thought about joining them, then let my gaze wander down the shed-row, past the nodding heads of the other horses, out to the dazzling sunshine at the end of the barn. Twenty more white barns, glowing in the sunlight, marched away along a tree-lined training track. Sunshine South was a lovely training center in the western reaches of civilization, just before solid land tipped into the water-meadows of the Everglades.

The Everglades seemed to influence the weather here, keeping the air sopping wet and the sun scorching, just the way the swamp liked it. Here it was mid-morning and already hot and humid; the Miami area had another climate completely from north Florida. It was still summer here, even if the calendar claimed it was already November. I fretted about the heat for a few moments. Personal Best ran okay in the heat, but I hadn't forgotten the night he'd been so sick in Saratoga—it had been hot then, too, while we waited for the weather to break and the rain to come at last. I wished we were back up at Tampa already, where the temperatures would be a little more sensible, and we were closer to home. I pushed Personal Best out of the stall door and peered in at his water bucket; it was half-empty.

"Good boy," I told him. "Stay hydrated." I didn't pull water buckets all day on race-days; it was too easy to allow a horse to get dehydrated in Florida.

My phone buzzed then; I looked down at it while Personal Best lipped at my hair, pulling strands from my pony tail. Sunshine South's security gate was calling. "Hello?"

"Got visitors here for Cotswold Farm?"

"Barn three," I said tightly.

"Gotta send an escort."

I sighed. "Be right there."

Have you ever seen someone light up, truly light up, as if there is an incandescent bulb suddenly switched on underneath their skin? When Wendy turned the corner and saw Personal Best, that's exactly what happened.

She was a plain little thing, with a pinched, nervous face. When I first saw her, she was clinging to the shirt of her chaperone—the aunt, I supposed. Her t-shirt had a picture of a sparkly pony on it; her pink leggings were a little baggy around her skinny legs. With red-brown hair pulled into a tight ponytail, highlighting that sharp little face, she reminded me of a frightened mouse. But I guessed she was just another poor rural kid, growing up in a rusty single-wide and wearing hand-me-downs. I felt a pang of sympathy, thinking of her and so many kids like her, the ones I saw every time I drove to the feed store or into town. *This* was why I didn't like kids, I realized, walking up to meet her. Because I hated to see their confusion and unhappiness when the world got too big and real. I hated seeing their dreams tempered by reality.

After a few awkward hellos, Wendy followed me back to the barn silently; her Aunt Karen, who appeared to be about twenty-one and utterly fascinated by whatever game she was playing on her phone, trailed behind. I took a couple quick glances behind me as we walked up the drive: Wendy was gazing around her with wide eyes, taking in the world of racehorses that she was excluded from back in Ocala; Karen flipped her finger across her phone and occasionally stumbled on a rough patch of asphalt.

Once in the barn, though, once she saw Personal Best, everything changed.

That pinched little face, nervous and suspicious and worried, became utterly illuminated. It was as if she was another person entirely. She stood still in the shed row, staring at Personal Best's white-blazed face while he regarded her calmly, her eyes wide and her mouth open, and we all just stopped in our tracks and watched her, impossibly moved by what we were seeing.

And then Personal Best neighed, shook his head, and disappeared into his stall.

That was his trick for *me*.

I stood still for a moment and tried to digest what had just happened. My colt was a traitor, that was what had just happened! How could he have whinnied like that for someone else?

But then I had to get over it and get moving: Wendy was already making a beeline for his stall door, and I had a feeling the little snot would dive under the webbing and dart right into the stall if I wasn't there to stop her. He might have told her something in that whinny, but it wasn't an invitation to go into his stall and wrap her skinny arms around his neck, I knew that much.

Sure enough, I grabbed Wendy by the arm just as she started to stoop under the webbing. "Easy there, princess," I drawled, dragging her back from the stall door. Inside, I could see Personal Best's hindquarters turned towards the door. Either he had expanded this trick to include all visitors (in hopes of getting more peppermints) or I had just been seriously betrayed. "No matter how nicely they talk to you, they don't want you in their house, okay? Trust me on this one."

She scowled up at me, and I was taken aback by the ferocity in her gaze. Though she be but little, she be fierce...from Shakespeare to my shed-row, that much was for certain. But this was a girl who had been made tough by misadventure, I reminded myself. She had been knocked around, and things were only getting worse. If she learned to fight for what she wanted, so much the better for her—just, it needed to be tempered with common sense.

"Listen up, Wendy," I said in a lower voice, so that the spectators behind us couldn't hear. "The best horsewoman in the world still has to learn her barn manners from someone older. So listen to me and I'll teach you what you need to know, okay?"

She regarded me sullenly for a moment, her hazel eyes boring into mine with an adult-like glare that was unsettling, to say the least. Then her features seemed to soften, as if she was letting go of tension, and she nodded. "I can listen," she muttered. "I want to learn."

I was a kid once. I know, I know, it's shocking. But I remembered—I remembered being a kid and being obsessed with horses and reading about them constantly and thinking that I knew what was up. And I remembered, suddenly, how mean I thought my first riding instructor was. The way she wouldn't let me do a thing without her hands on mine. The way I couldn't make a move without her permission, her supervision, her constant instruction. And the way I somehow, without knowing it, not only stopped resenting her for that, but stopped needing her for that. She knew when it was safe to let me go, let me get hurt a little, without scaring me away from horses forever.

I needed that wisdom now. I was a trainer; now I needed to be a teacher. I could teach a kid, just like I trained a horse, right?

Start small, see what the horse knows already.

"Have you ever touched a horse before?" I asked Wendy, who crinkled her brow in response. "I'm not going to tell on you," I added.

"My neighbors have horses," she whispered, casting a sidelong glance at her aunt, who was standing with her arms folded, watching us suspiciously. "I'm not allowed. But I've petted them. And…I've gotten on one's back. He didn't do nothing."

"Oh Wendy," I whispered, joining in with her spirit of conspiracy. "You're so bad!" And I grinned to take the edge off the accusation. "Don't do that anymore, okay? You need to learn how to handle horses safely or you could get hurt, right?"

Wendy nodded slowly. "He didn't do nothing," she repeated. And then, resolutely: "Okay. I'll listen."

"So here's what you're going to do…" I took her hand in mine and put a peppermint in her flat palm, slipping it out of its plastic wrapper as I did so.

Personal Best immediately turned his head, ears pricked. I crinkled the wrapper again and he was heading for the door in an instant. "Pig," I giggled, and Wendy did the same. The laughter seemed to relax her; she let me take hold of her fingers and bend them backwards so that there was no way they could end up in the colt's mouth. "And here we go—"

I put her palm up to Personal Best as he leaned over the webbing and *crunch* went the peppermint, his teeth just scraping at her palm as he snatched it. Wendy's eyes widened but she didn't move; I had to lower her hand for her. She seemed to have lost the ability to speak or move on her own.

"So, that's how it's done," I said, moving her back a step or two so that the colt couldn't dribble minty drool on her pink pony t-shirt. "You fed Personal Best his favorite candy."

Wendy's face was a sight to see: something between ecstasy and terror. That's horses, I thought. That's working with horses in a nutshell.

Chapter Four

AFTER THAT THINGS BECAME more interesting. My nerves relaxed, and I settled into my teaching role with pleasure. I had a few hours before we had to get Personal Best over to the track, and Alexander and Brian were more than capable of making sure the gear was ready to go and the horse was tidy, so I decided to give the kid a thorough look at my world.

I started seeing the day with the racehorses through a more wondering lens, taking in the striking beauty of the everyday sights I had grown accustomed to. The steam rising from the backs of hot horses as they were bathed after their work-outs, the pattern of footfalls on concrete as horses were jogged up and checked for soundness in the parking lot in front of the barn, the constant rumble of nickers and shrill whinnies, the shouts from riders as young horses danced and jigged and hopped in their athletic excitement. The racetrack, the farm, the training center: they were the backdrop of my life, and so their charms had grown questionable as the daily grind took over the enchantment of finding myself in the places I had once dreamed of. But it was all new for Wendy, and her very delight was thrilling to me.

"What's that?" she asked about everything in the tack room, as I pointed out the training yokes, the different bits, the latex wraps, the wickedly long safety pins we used on bandages. "What's it for?" was even better—explaining how the yoke helped riders keep young horses straight and in line, how the neckstrap was like a little extra security handle, how Velcro fastenings might become loose and dangerous when a horse was galloping and so we used bandage pins to keep their wraps safely in place. She'd read books, that much was obvious—she understood bridles and snaffle bits and girths and saddles. But there isn't much literature for kids about horse racing, and however much it looks like English riding with very small saddles—it isn't.

When we were done touring the shed-row, she asked if she could get on a horse.

I looked apprehensively at her aunt, who was sitting on a straw bale scrolling through her phone. Every few moments she reached down and scratched at the back of her thighs, where the straw was irritating all the skin exposed by her very short skirt. She wasn't paying attention the our conversation. I'd get no help from that quarter.

"I don't have anyone for you to ride here," I explained, turning back to Wendy. "These are all racehorses, and they're not safe for you to ride. Plus we have to get ready to take Personal Best to the racetrack now."

Her face fell again. "I thought I could ride a horse."

I had told Linda *specifically* to tell them I didn't have a pony to put her on, and Linda had said that was all taken care of. Obviously, that hadn't been communicated. "Today's for watching horses," I said desperately. "*I'm* not even riding a horse today."

"Alex?" Alexander was standing at the top of the shed row with Brian, a bucket in hand and a cooler over his arm. "The van is going to be here any minute. Are you ready?"

I turned; Personal Best was leaning out, nosing around for any stray bits of hay leftover from the hay-net the grooms had taken away from him earlier. There was a big manure stain on his hip—he'd taken a nap while we'd been looking around the barn. I should have told a groom to tie him. "Um," I said, pointing.

"What?" Alexander came down the shed and looked. "I need a groom!" he called to Brian. "Some alcohol and a rag!"

Brian came himself, casting me a baleful glance as he ducked into the stall and started rubbing at the manure stain with a towel, spraying on rubbing alcohol to draw the greenish-brown mark out of the colt's shining red coat. I shrugged helplessly; Alexander, holding the colt's halter, shook his head at me: *ignore it*. I nodded, but I was starting to feel irritated again at having to drag this kid around with me on a racing day. Any other day might have been fine, but today I needed my wits about me, not distracted by amusing little Miss Wendy.

"I need you to go back with your aunt for a while," I told her.

Wendy fixed me with a fierce expression. "I want to go with *you.*"

"I have to get Personal Best ready for his race, Wendy. I can't think about anything but him."

"Why?"

"Because I have to watch every step he takes to make sure he's perfectly sound. I have to see every time he sneezes or coughs or shakes his head. If I don't send him out to the track one hundred percent perfect, he could get hurt."

That got her attention. Evidently, Wendy was no stranger to racing tragedy caught on camera. "Like fall down and get hurt?" Her voice was thinner, worried.

"Maybe."

She nodded slowly. "Okay. I understand."

It hurt to watch her walk slowly across the shed-row to where her bored aunt was sitting on the straw bale, tugging at her arm to get the young woman's attention. It was obvious she was used to being left on the sidelines, but she still didn't like it, for all that it was part of her life. I wanted more for her, so much that it hurt. I felt an ache in my stomach as her aunt nodded and went back to her phone, and it did a little flip-flop when she settled herself on the straw bale and looked at me, her face resigned.

But I had a job to do. I waggled my fingers at her and went over to Personal Best's stall, trying to get my head together and my game face on. A groom came over with wraps and handed them over, and I ducked under the webbing, with Alexander still at his head, so I could do up his shipping bandages myself.

It was a soothing process, a ritual really, that put me in tune with my horse. I did up his legs one by one, thick pillow wraps covered by stiffer nylon bandages, safety-pinned into place, to keep him protected from hock and knee right down to the hoof. I took a horsehair brush from the groom and ran it over his coat slowly, almost reverently, knocking away the dust from the straw as I checked his entire body for any sort of swelling, any source of heat, any touch of soreness which we might have missed somehow in a hundred similar groomings and inspections. And then I took the chain shank, ran it over his nose, and waited for Alexander to drop the webbing so that we could go marching out of the stall, down the shed-row, and to the loading dock, where we'd walk up an earthen ramp and into the belly of the waiting horse van.

I did all that and felt calmer, restored to myself, close to Personal Best. He breathed his hot breath on my fingers in the van while I leaned against the half-door, looking out at the south Florida traffic, watching the surprised faces on tourists and locals alike as they saw a human and a horse in the tractor-trailer next to them. I rode with one arm hooked around the bar in front of Personal Best's chest so that I wouldn't fall in the stop-and-start interstate motion, or the constant red lights as we neared the racetrack, the trailer rattling over the bumps and grinds of Florida's always-crumbling roads.

Sometimes Alexander pulled up alongside us in the farm SUV and I would wave to him and blow kisses and act generally ridiculous, and he would shake his head and smile at me, while appreciative drivers from nearby cars blew their horns and cat-called with typical Floridian chivalry. It was all part of the ritual, this drive from Sunshine South's pastoral quiet out amongst the Everglades to the hustle and bustle of the city track, the bright white tropical light bathing the beachside condominiums in a shimmering glow, while inside the truck it was still country, sawdust on the floor and hot sweet horse breath in my ear.

And when we pulled up at the loading dock on the backside, I was ready, and so was Personal Best.

Chapter Five

ALL THROUGH THE PADDOCK and the strut out to the racetrack I was trying not to notice her, but Wendy was always there, as close as she could manage to creep before either Alexander or Brian would grab at her and send her back to stand by her aunt. She shouldn't have been anywhere near the saddling stalls at all. We had invited her into the paddock to watch with the understanding that she stay near the center of the enclosure with all the other guests who didn't know enough not to get trampled by a horse: the syndicate owners with their cigars and their wives in stilettos, the families dressed up as if it was Easter Sunday brunch, the sullen teenage daughter dragged along and hunched over in a frumpy dress bought special for the occasion while she wished she were anywhere but amidst all the glitz and glitter of these wealthy (mostly older) celebrants here to celebrate their tax shelters on four legs.

But of course that wasn't good enough for Wendy, who was probably used to taking what she wanted since no one was ever going to give it to her, and she would dart away from her bored aunt at every occasion, taking advantage of the young woman's total preoccupation with her phone. I'd step backwards only to trip over Wendy, who hadn't been there a moment before. Then Brian or Alexander would step forward and pull her away so that I could go on with whatever I had been doing: talking to the jockey, tightening the over-girth, having a heart-to-heart with Personal Best.

But honestly, the kid was so underfoot it was a wonder I didn't boost *her* into the saddle instead of the jockey.

And trust me, she would have loved that.

I pulled her close after I came back from walking Personal Best to the outrider. "Come on, kid," I told her, snatching her hand. "Let's go to the track."

When I pushed through the crowd along the rail, nudging aside a cigar-smoking gent who was blocking the opening to the track, she stayed gamely close to me, her eyes wide as she saw where we were going. Right out onto the racetrack, our feet in the dirt where her heroes galloped, to lean against the railing and look casual along with the grooms waiting to catch their horses after the race.

A security guard glanced over at her. "You can't have a kid out here," he said disapprovingly. "No one under eighteen, come on now."

I put her right in the gap and pushed her a little bit, until she was standing just behind the railing. "How's that?"

He didn't look happy with me, but he let it slide.

"If a racehorse goes out of control and starts running this way, go all the way behind the rail, okay?"

Wendy nodded, eyes like saucers. But her skinny face was excited anyway; she wasn't really that afraid of being run over by a horse, I could tell. The kid thought she was an expert when she arrived this morning; now that she had fed a racehorse a peppermint and survived the paddock, she probably thought she was ready for her trainer's license.

I liked that. I remembered that. Confidence for absolutely no reason, that was something I missed about my pre-equestrian childhood. Before I found out that falling off hurts and that someone older always knows more than you.

I squeezed her hand and then, on an impulse, hung Personal Best's halter off her shoulder. "Now you look like a real groom," I told her. "I'd make you carry the bucket, too, but it'll just make your arm tired."

And pinch-faced little Wendy beamed.

"The horses are in the gate for the Loxahatchee Stakes!"

I stiffened. Wendy stiffened. I could see it in her shoulders when I looked back to check on her, the way her fingers were gripping the bucket—she had taken it from me after all, to really feel like a groom—and in the hard line of her jaw. She was scared. I reached back and took her free hand, giving it a good squeeze.

"We got this, honey," I told her, and then wondered why I would say such a ridiculous thing; before a horse race, no one had *anything*. It was the most helpless moment in a trainer's life, waiting for their horse to come home safe.

But it made Wendy feel better, anyway; she nodded resolutely and shifted her weight a little, the tension dropping out of her shoulders. We looked down the track to where the horses were about to burst out and run past us; when they came around a second time, they'd be pulling up, their races run.

The bell rang and the doors flew backwards; the horses came charging out of the gate with the slapping of leather and the shouting of jockeys that you didn't hear on most television broadcasts. It was a raw, rare thing, and Wendy leaned forward, craning her head to see around me, though I kept her safely behind the the railing. The ground rumbled as the hooves came pounding down the track towards us, and I strained to see Personal Best's white face in the pack of horses as they approached. Then they were racing past us, tightly bunched along the rail, the dirt flying up in a cloud behind them, and heading into the clubhouse turn almost before we could register what we were seeing.

"Where is he?" Wendy asked urgently, her voice high and nervous.

The loudspeaker was echoing terribly where we were standing, so I checked the giant LED screen that dominated the infield. Finally I saw him, tucked well back in fifth or sixth on the rail, running steadily in tight company. "He's there in the middle," I told her, pointing. "And it's a slow steady pace, so he'll have to find room and close like a madman, or he won't be able to get to the front in time."

"What does that mean?"

"It mean the horse in front is purposely going slowly so that he can take off really fast in the homestretch and trick everyone." I watched the screen anxiously now; they were deep in the backstretch and no one was shifting position, but if for some reason any one of the three horses running in front of Personal Best were to slow down dramatically, he'd be in a pretty bad position, having to either look for room to get around the horse in very tight quarters, or slow down himself and lose valuable momentum and rhythm.

"Does he get scared with all those other horses so close?" Wendy asked, squinting at the screen.

"No baby," I said thoughtlessly. "Just the humans do."

"Are you scared?"

"No," I lied. "Everything is fine."

The horses swept into the final turn with very little change, and then the two horses on the lead launched into high gear, their jockeys rocking on their backs and swinging their sticks frantically, each one trying to draw clear of the other. But the two leaders were either very evenly matched or very into one another; they ran neck and neck, heads bobbing in unison, with no one challenging them from behind, for a very long time. Or what seemed like a very long time. Personal Best was still trapped behind the laboring horse running in third, with another horse's saddle-cloth just right of his nose; he was utterly trapped until the horse on his right either made a move or stopped.

They were in the final furlong now, they were nearing the sixteenth pole. The horse in front of Personal Best seemed to be falling into slow motion; he was stopping; Personal Best would be stopped too.

I reacted like any trainer would, with a cry to the racing gods. "Get out of our way! We're not even going to make it into the money, for fuck's sake!"

I'd forgotten Wendy was there.

But I wasn't the only one. All around me the grooms, the fans on the apron, the players in the stands were in full cry, drowning out the echoing race call, the cries of the ever-present seagulls, the drumming of the horses' hooves as they came to the final sixteenth of the race. They were screaming, they were cursing, they were urging their horses on and damning their horses to hell, men and women and gamblers and socialites alike, clamoring to make their horse come home first.

And that was when Personal Best put his white face around the doddering horse to his right, his head turned nearly ninety degrees by his desperate jock, and started his charge.

"*Goddammit get a move on Personal Best!*" I shrieked, lending my voice to the masses, adding my obscenity-laced prayers to the thousands of others being thrown up to heaven as the horses thundered towards the final pole. "*Fucking run, goddammit, get him up there! Get on!*"

And beside me, I heard a shrill piping voice rising up to join the chorus: "*Fucking run, goddammit! Fucking run! You got this Personal Best! RUN!*"

And when he put his face in front in the final strides and won the Loxahatchee Stakes by the barest whisker, I leaned down and gave that little cuss a big kiss on her forehead.

Chapter Six

I WAS TOO SWEPT up in watching Personal Best walking back to the barn to remember to tell Wendy to watch her mouth, but she was a quick study of audiences, and by the time I got to her, standing near the wash area outside the barn where she'd been watching me hose the sweat and track dirt off of the colt, squeezing a sponge over his poll and whipping the water out of his tail, she had already been trying out her new words with one of Brian's grooms, who thought she was hysterical.

"He fucking ran them down," she was explaining to the groom, a round-faced Puerto Rican man of about sixty who was slapping his knee and telling her to go on, go on, go on. "He ran like a fucking freight train."

"Wendy!" I called, running over to the pair. I looked around for her aunt; but as usual the so-called chaperone was deeply involved with some text conversation. The chick lived in her phone, I swore. And speaking of swearing: "You have to stop talking like that. You're going to get me into trouble."

The groom just laughed, his shoulders shaking. Wendy scowled. "I want to be a racetracker," she announced. "Like you."

I couldn't help but be touched by that, I admit. And for a moment, I savored the words. After all, who doesn't want to be a role model, a hero even? I had very few female heroines as a racehorse-obsessed child: Julie Krone was the most visible woman in the industry, and she was a jockey—a job I knew wasn't for me from a fairly young age. Female trainers? If there were any when I was a kid, I certainly didn't know about them. And so here was a little girl, looking up and saying she wanted to be *like me*...I felt, for a few moments anyway, like I was somebody.

Just, somebody who swore a lot. I shook my head and pulled myself together. This kid's grandmother probably wasn't going to think much of her granddaughter's new role model if the most noticeable change I created was a potty-mouth. "I would love for you to be a racetracker," I said carefully. "But maybe you could be a new kind of racetracker, who doesn't cuss quite as much as we do."

The groom wiped tears out of his eyes. "You can't be talkin' that way," he told her. "You make people laugh, they can't do their work. We got a lotta work to do, you know? Can't be distracted by some cute little princess who talks like a man."

Wendy was not impressed. "*She's* a woman and she talks like that," she informed the groom. "It's not talking like a man."

"She do talk like a man," the groom said with a shrug. "But it ain't funny."

I had a feeling my femininity was being assaulted here, but I also wasn't sure I had any femininity to assault, at least nothing that I put on display. I didn't own any skirts, heels, or make-up, and if a man tried to take a straw bale or a feed bag from me I generally had a fit and told him to mind his own damned business. "It's talking like a *grown-up*," I corrected, and took Wendy's hand. "And that's just going to have to wait until you're grown-up."

We went into the barn, considering the case closed, and Wendy immediately went to see Luna, who was looking over her webbing, waiting for Personal Best to come back to his stall so that she could squeal and kick the wall between them. The filly took one look at the girl and ducked back into her stall, swishing her tail irritably. Wendy looked forlorn. "She doesn't like me."

"She doesn't like strangers," I lied. This was interesting, I thought, leaning over the webbing and clucking my tongue at Luna, who flicked an ear in response and then stamped her hind leg with evident irritation. Personal Best had treated Wendy like family from the get-go, but Luna didn't want anything to do with her. What had initially looked like a natural knack with horses was apparently a more selective thing. Some people seemed to have an aura that just attracted all horses, but evidently Wendy didn't.

Personal Best, on the other hand, nickered a greeting to Wendy as he was led past, making his rounds of the shed-row as he was being walked dry. Wendy's face lit up again at the horse's obvious affection for her. "Why does he do that? Does he know I love him?"

"That must be it," I said, but I really didn't know either.

Suddenly Luna was back at her webbing and looking out of the barn, her head high and her ears pricked. I turned around to see what had grabbed her attention and saw a dark little horse being led into the barn.

"Who's that?" Wendy asked.

"Must be for another trainer in the barn," I said, watching the horse, who was unimpressive. As the pair neared us, I saw the slightly dished profile and wide eyes that often marked a filly, the dainty ankles and dished hooves of a horse who had spent a lot of time in sand, and a slender chest that didn't say a lot for her power or strength. Just another Thoroughbred, probably Florida-bred, running in claiming races before she went back to some little backyard in Florida to be a broodmare, I figured. Categorized and dismissed, I nodded at the groom as he went by and went back to playing with Luna's mane.

But then the groom stopped. The filly on his lead-shank stopped too, blinked at me, and then turned her nervous gaze on Wendy, who smiled at the attention. The brass name plate on her halter read *Christmasfordee*. The groom, a tiny middle-aged Hispanic man with broad cheeks and a bristling mustache, just looked at me with unblinking eyes.

"You looking for someone?" I asked finally.

He shifted on his feet before speaking in heavily accented English. "You know Cotswold? I look for trainer."

I cocked my head. What the hell was this? "I'm their trainer," I said, even though he was probably looking for Brian.

"Okay, I got horse for you." He made to hand me the shank, but I put my hands up instead.

"What do you mean? I don't have any horses coming in."

The groom's expression didn't change. "My boss sell this horse, guy say, take to Cotswold in barn three. He say that he trainer."

Oh jeez. Oh hell. Oh sweet baby Jesus. "Wendy!" I snapped, suddenly noticing that the kid was reaching up to touch the dark filly's nose. The filly was reaching towards her, ears pricked and mouth working, as if she was anticipating a treat. "Don't touch strange horses. That's a great way to lose your fingers." Wendy, her face darkening, put her hands behind her back, but she stayed close to the filly.

I turned back to the groom. "Look, I know you're just doing what you're told, but I need some paperwork or something on this. I can't just accept a horse without even knowing who she belongs to. You're going to have to call your boss or go get him before I can take this horse."

"Listen, lady—" the groom started, his bland expression starting to fold into anger, but he was interrupted from a shout at the other end of the shed. We both turned and saw a tall, almost hilariously thin figure coming down the aisle towards us.

I shook my head. I should've known.

"That him," the groom muttered. "Owner."

"Of course it is. Joey!" I called in a more civil tone. "Joey, what did you do?" I smiled, as if it was all in good fun, and I wasn't utterly seething with rage at seeing that he'd done it again.

"I'm sorry, Alex," he laughed, spreading his hands as he came near. Bumbling Joey Armstrong, his gesture said, the silly fool you can't help but love. He thought he was living in a sitcom from the fifties. "I just fell in love with her cute little face. I had to have her! You have a stall for her, don't you?"

Joey Armstrong, who owned a car dealership empire, frequently fell in love with horses and their cute little faces. He was less attracted to things like bullet works or race records or clean vet charts, unfortunately. I wondered how many problems his current heartthrob had, and how long it would be before we instructed Brian to drop her into a claimer and get her out of our barn. Or, even worse, find that she was fundamentally unsound and have to tell Joey that his little sweetheart was a breakdown waiting to happen and needed to be retired immediately. That was what had happened with his last horse, a five-year-old maiden named Chippewasintrouble, a name that was nearly impossible to pronounce correctly without patient instruction, and who was definitely not worth the time said instruction took. His new owner, a teenager who was training him to barrel race, wisely lengthened it to Chippewa's In Trouble and seemed to be happy with its western connotations.

"Joey," I said carefully, trying not to sound as angry as I was. "Didn't we talk about checking with your trainer before you buy another horse?"

Joey didn't even blink, let alone drop his smile. "Yes," he said in a mischievous voice, like a toddler who is pretty sure he's not actually in trouble. "But I knew once you saw her, you wouldn't be mad. She's too sweet."

I glanced back at the filly and her big troubled eyes. She had a broad, oversized nasal bone which gave her profile a coarse look. I was missing the sweetness, apparently. I must be too cynical to see it. Wendy on the other hand...Wendy was watching the mare like she'd just spotted her soul-mate across the room and was too shy to introduce herself.

"I don't even know if there *are* any stalls," I went on. "I don't know if the one next to Luna's is ours or the other trainer's."

"Oh, I'm sure you'll find room," Joey said confidently. "You always find room for me."

That might be the problem, I thought.

"What's going on here?"

Problem might be solved.

Alexander came around the corner with Brian and Personal Best, the colt still working at some grass from his special bonus grazing session. "Joey Armstrong, is that you?"

Joey *was* pretty recognizable, since he was probably six and a half feet tall and had the physique of a grasshopper. Even so, he behaved as if Alexander was a clairvoyant from a freak show. "Alexander! How did you guess? It's getting so dark—you should really turn the lights on," he told me in an aside, before turning back to the advancing Alexander.

It might have been getting dark, but I could still see Alexander's face, and it was not pleased. I had a feeling I was about to see an owner get fired. "Hey Wendy?"

She dragged fascinated eyes away from the filly and looked at me with obvious irritation. This filly *was* trouble; she had everyone in a bad mood. Everyone but Joey. I plastered a fake smile on my face. "Why don't we go find your aunt? We're going to be headed out soon and she'd probably like to get back to her hotel before dark. That way you guys can get rested and see the beach in the morning. Sounds nice, right?"

Wendy obviously didn't think the beach sounded nice at all, because she rolled her eyes and sighed heavily. But I didn't care; she didn't need to be here for Alexander's inevitable meltdown with Joey, nor the things he was going to say about the filly she was apparently head-over-heels in love with.

I started to take her hand and lead her away, but the filly took a step after her, nickering. *That's odd*, I thought, but I didn't have much time to ponder the move, because the groom's over-the-top reaction, yanking down on the chain shank over her nose and letting lose a string of Spanish obscenities, caused Wendy to shriek and shove the man in the gut, knocking him right over.

He rolled in the dirt of the shed-row, though thankfully not under the filly, who responded to the debacle by rearing straight up, her lead shank dangling between her legs. I lunged forward to try and get at the shank, but the cussing groom was in my way; I tripped and went to my knees, and when I looked up, Wendy had the shank in her hands and was talking soothingly to the filly, who was crab-stepping nervously away from the pair of us in the dirt.

Behind it all, Alexander had his arms out, as if to shield Personal Best and Brian should the filly spin and take off down the shed-row, and Joey was just standing there with his mouth hanging open.

Like so many equine accidents, everything happened so quickly there was scarcely time to react until after the fact. I picked myself up slowly, brushing the dirt from my slacks, and made my way towards Wendy, eyes on the filly's wide eyes, which were rolling white in her homely head. "Honey, hand me the shank, okay?"

"No," Wendy said gently, and continued talking to the filly in the same soft tone she'd been using before. "That's a good girl, stand still now, don't worry—"

"Wendy, come on, you could get hurt." I put my hand out; Wendy moved the shank out of my reach. Her total attention was on the horse, but just as the wary filly was keeping one ear trained on me, Wendy was definitely aware of me—and apparently saw me as a threat.

"She's scared," Wendy said. "She likes me; we'll be fine."

"Come on, little girl," Joey said. "Give Alex the lead shank. That's a racehorse. She might take off and then what will happen to you?"

"She won't," Wendy insisted.

I shook my head in irritation and darted my hand forward, snatching the shank before Wendy could stop me. "That's enough, kid," I snapped. "Go find your aunt like I said."

Wendy gave me a sorrowful look, as if I'd betrayed her and run over her dog in the bargain. Then she stepped up and gave the filly a long, careful stroke down her trembling dark neck, running her hands beneath the black mane where it spilled over her sharp withers. Then, without a word, she turned and walked out of the shed-row, off to find her texting aunt, just as I'd told her.

I sighed and gave the filly a pat. "Let's walk," I told her, still sensing that a loud argument was brewing behind me, and took her for a stroll around the barn while her groom sat in the dirt and her owner started pleading his case with Alexander.

Chapter Seven

WE WENT BACK TO our condo that night, the old beachfront job that Alexander had been using for south Florida racing since the nineties. It had been old then, and now its comfortingly outdated furnishings and fittings were some of my favorite things. I loved the marble windowsills and the plastic and chrome bathroom fixtures, the louvered windows and the white Formica kitchen cabinets. It all reminded me of friends' houses when I was a kid. Chrome and white, plastic and nickel: mid-century Florida definitely had its own look.

The carpet was always damp and the linoleum in the kitchen was starting to peel, too. Those parts, I didn't love, although they were still an undeniable part of Florida.

Alexander was sitting with a glass of wine on the balcony, watching the Atlantic Ocean come crashing ashore in the moonlight. There was a cruise ship on the horizon, lit up like a Christmas tree. I came out and shut the sliding glass door behind me, letting the humid salty air rise up to meet me, and watched the ship for a moment. "We should go on a cruise," I suggested. "I've never done that."

Alexander shrugged. "Who has the time?"

"True." I sat down next to him. "Did you call Jackson?" Jackson Hicks was a trainer friend; Alexander had suggested, after the shouting had ended and things were more civil, that Joey should take the filly to his barn. He was adamant that we weren't taking the horse into our string; she was a four-year-old maiden who was unplaced in three starts and had needed a lengthy break between each race, for reasons unknown to us. Jackson had both open stalls and a remarkable capacity for dealing with delusional owners, so we figured she'd be safe with him. In a few months, with any luck, the filly would be heading for retirement. Hopefully not as a broodmare, I thought, remembering her dished hooves and narrow chest. She wasn't exactly the face of future champions. With careful shoeing, though, she could probably make a decent show horse.

"I left him a voicemail." He took a sip of wine and then picked up an empty glass he'd had waiting. "Sit a while?"

I sat down next to him, settling into the rickety plastic chair that had been on this balcony for the past twenty years, and accepted the glass. Alexander poured with an artistic flourish, topping off the glass with a bob of his hand, and then raised his own glass for a toast. "To Personal Best, and his beautiful trainer," he said with a smile that crinkled his face into a thousand sun-darkened lines. "May you always find the finish line first, my love."

I sniffed and blinked away a suspicious burning in my eyes. "Thank you, Alexander," I said throatily. "I couldn't have done it without you." We clinked glasses, the little crystal *ping* echoing around the three walls of the balcony, and drank. I watched the ocean in silence for a little while, wondering what sort of creatures were just below the surface. Sharks, probably, and crabs, and jellyfish. But maybe pretty things, as well, tropical fish and coral reefs, dolphins and seahorses. "Do dolphins sleep at night?" I asked, and Alexander laughed and said he genuinely had no idea and had never wondered about such a thing in his life.

"I would have thought you'd be thinking about your horses," he went on. "What you want to do next with Personal Best."

"I still plan on bringing him home."

"And next year?"

"We'll see how he does after a month off."

"Are you thinking about it?"

I was silent for a moment. I knew what he was getting at—it was what everyone was always thinking about, in this business, anyway. And anytime you had a two-year-old with guts and speed and a couple stakes wins under his belt, you *had* to think about it. "Yes," I admitted.

He nodded. The waves roared. "I won't be mad," he said finally.

"You won't be mad?"

"If you win a Derby before I do."

I burst out laughing and leaned over to kiss him.

Later that evening, past the time that anyone should have been calling anyone—okay, I was watching the ten o'clock news— my phone buzzed, skidding its way across the glass coffee table and hitting the beige carpet with a clunk. I picked it up, looked at the number, and then just shook my head. It was Wendy's aunt's phone, but all bets were that it was Wendy calling.

I went out onto the balcony before answering. Sure enough, it was Wendy. "Alex?" she said in a hushed voice.

"What's up, Wendy?" The cruise ship had moved well out into the ocean; it was nearly gone, just a faint glimmer of light on the horizon now.

"I was worried about Christmas."

"Christmas?" Christmas was more than six weeks away. And I didn't recall any promises to be part of her Christmas, or even part of her life after today. The Rodeo Queens were taking care of her riding lessons. It was up to Wendy to learn how to ride, maybe even show, and then when she was an adult she could start thinking about being a racetracker, if that was what she still wanted.

"The *filly*," Wendy explained impatiently. "The one you don't want."

"Oh. Wait—Christmas?" I thought for a moment, trying to remember when anyone had called the filly by name. Then I remembered: the dull glint of brass on her leather halter, the Roman letters proclaimed her *Christmasfordee*. "That might not even be her name," I said. "That could be an old halter. We reuse halters all the time."

"No, that's her name," Wendy asserted. "I asked that mean man. When you walked her away. I said I was sorry even though I wasn't, and then I asked her name. He said they called her Christmas. In the barn. When she races her name is Christmasfordee."

I didn't know if what she did could accurately be called *racing*. "She'll be fine," I said instead. "She'll go to a friend of ours and he'll do the right thing for her."

"I want *you* to keep her," Wendy insisted, her voice fretful. "I want to be able to see her. Can you bring her back to your farm and keep her there? I can work to help pay for her. I can do whatever you need."

What on earth? "No, I can't do that. She isn't my horse, Wendy. She has an owner. He just wants a trainer for her, you know? She has to stay at the racetrack until he changes his mind."

"But—" Wendy's voice was trembling and I was afraid she was going to cry. If Wendy cried, I cried; it was that simple. "But she's special. She has my name, and it's almost Christmas, and—"

"She has your name?"

"My Nana calls me Dee."

"Oh." Well, this was really, really unfortunate. Now I could see what had happened. Girl on Christmas wish trip is suddenly presented with a horse whose name literally implies the horse is her Christmas present. Girl falls in love with horse. What an unfortunate little strike of fortune. "Wendy, honey, you're not ready to own a horse yet, okay? I know you want one but you *have* to take lessons and learn to ride and take care of them. That's your next step—learning everything you can. I know this horse had a name that sounded like she was for you, but—"

"No," Wendy interrupted. "That's not what I meant. I know I can't have her. But she's *special.* I could see she was special. And she's scared. And we have the same name—that has to mean something."

I stared out at the sea. The cruise ship had disappeared; the ocean was dark at last. Down on the beach, ten stories below, a couple were walking hand-in-hand, not a care in the world. Up here on the balcony, I had a phone call with an eleven-year-old having a New Age moment with a slow racehorse. I wished, very hard, to be anywhere but here, with any other problem. Nothing changed.

"Wendy," I said slowly. "Listen. You have to go to bed. It's late, you had a long day, you have a long trip home tomorrow. Don't worry about the horse. I'll make sure she goes to a good home."

Alexander favored me with one of his eloquently arched eyebrows. "But she will ride a broodmare around the pasture with nothing but a halter and a lead-rope."

I shook my head. "No idea."

He grunted and sat down at the breakfast table with the training ledger. We sat in silence for a while, a rare quiet afternoon in the middle of a farm that never ceased its demands. A Christmas song came on the radio, playing tinnily from atop the fridge in the kitchen. Alexander started humming along. It took me a moment to name it—*Winter Wonderland*. A funny song, for Ocala. *I've Been Dreaming of a Brown Christmas*, that would be more accurate. Christmas on my mind, I considered the seasonal necessity of ordering turkeys and putting the velveteen ribbons on the farm gates. Just add it to the to-do list, already a hundred miles long.

I tried to pretend there weren't a thousand things I could be doing out in the barns, and that I wasn't nervous about the way Alexander's brow creased as he ran his finger down the hand-written training notes and times. But he finally closed the book with a sigh and a satisfied nod. I read a book review about a history of Florida and highlighted the name of it, as if a history book was something I was going to have the time and brain cells to read.

The phone rang.

Alexander looked at me. "You're on phone duty until I say otherwise."

I got up and dragged myself to the wall. It was my own fault. "Cotswold!" I announced cheerfully, making a face at Alexander. "This is Alex! Who is this!"

Alexander shook his head at me, as if there was no hope for me and he had given up entirely. I smiled.

"Alex? It's me—it's Wendy."

My smile flipped into a frown.

"Hi, Wendy," I replied warily. Not that she wasn't a cute kid, but I had been hoping I'd heard the last of Wendy. I didn't have time to be a big sister, after all, and the Rodeo Queens were supposed to be setting her up with a local hunter/jumper trainer to teach her riding lessons. I'd assumed she was someone else's problem now. "What's up?"

"I was wondering..." She hesitated. "I was wondering if I could come over."

"Come over...*here?*"

"Um...yes?"

"Why? I mean—what do you want to do?"

"Hang out with you?" She sounded timid, as if she was second-guessing her decision.

"Hang out with me?" I repeated, baffled.

I looked around the kitchen as if the cabinets held some sort of wisdom. Specifically, a way to tell this kid no way, she could not come over, we were not going to be buddies in an upcoming 80s-style zany comedy. Alexander help up a finger: *hang on a minute.*

"Hold on, Wendy, okay?" I said urgently, and put my hand over the receiver. "What?"

"She can ride Betsy," Alexander whispered. "Tell her she can come over one afternoon and the two of you can go riding."

"She doesn't ride," I whispered back, not even ready to digest the fact that Alexander was allowing some kid he barely knew to ride his beloved Betsy. "She needs lessons. I'm not qualified to teach her anything."

"Teach her to hack and have fun," he suggested. "Let someone else teach her the hard stuff. She needs to just enjoy herself, too. The kid's had a hard life. Give her a couple hours. You might have fun, too."

I nodded slowly. He was right. I'd had fun with Wendy last Saturday, at least when I'd been free to show her around, give her the tour, answer her questions. I'd like the way she'd looked up to me. I didn't get that a lot. "Thanks, Alexander," I said, and I meant it.

I uncovered the phone. "Wendy? How would you like to come have a ride with me on a real racetrack?"

Alexander went on humming the Christmas song.

She looked so cute on Betsy I could hardly stand it. "You were born to ride," I told her admiringly. "Look at those legs."

Wendy's face lit up in that astonishing way that it had, and my heart squeezed. I loved seeing her happy. "Do you mean it?" she breathed.

"Absolutely. I mean everything I say." And it was true: Wendy's gangly body just *worked* on a horse. Her long skinny legs reached far down Betsy's barrel; her slim little upper-body was ram-rod straight in the Western saddle, and her hands were holding the reins gently and with empathy, not gripping them tightly with nerves and lack of experience. She looked like she'd been riding all her life. "Are you sure this is the first time you've ridden a horse?"

"With a saddle," Wendy giggled, and I remembered her telling me about jumping on the ponies in the pasture next to her house. I had to grin.

"Well, let's walk around the shed-row to start," I suggested. "Just like we're taking the horses out in the morning." Leaving her with Betsy to wait in the aisle, I took Parker, already tacked up, out of his stall and swung into the saddle. I came up next to Betsy and slipped a leather strap through her bit. "Now I'm ponying you, like you're on a rotten baby who can't be trusted on his own." Wendy giggled again, and then shut up very quickly when we started walking forward. I saw her bite her lip in concentration, trying to figure out how to move with the horse's motion.

"Just loosen your body and let her swing you around a little," I suggested. "Don't worry about how you look, worry about how you feel. Your fancy hunter trainer will teach you how to look."

"Okay," Wendy said stiffly. "I can do that. She moves more than I thought she would."

"Wait until you gallop."

Wendy just grinned, clearly in love with the thought.

We made our way around the shed-row a few times and then I suggested we walk down to the racetrack and do a loop. "Just at a walk," I added, seeing her face pale a little behind its deep tan. "Betsy already worked today and she's not in any hurry."

When we were done with the ride, I showed Wendy how to untack the horse and give her a shower. The November day was warm and Betsy's coat was long, ready for fast-moving cold fronts and sudden freezes, so it took a while to get the sweat out of all that fur. By the end of the shower, Wendy was soaked and filthy. I told her she looked like a true horsewoman now, and was rewarded with another one of those brilliant smiles. I was starting to like having this kid around.

I walked her up to the house to wait for her aunt to come and pick her up. According to Wendy, her grandma was too tired all the time to drive her places. "But she's going to feel better after Christmas," Wendy assured me. "That's what she told me. That's when her medicine will start working."

I didn't know what was going on with Wendy's grandmother, and I didn't want to know. But I sincerely hoped that if anything happened to the poor woman, the kid wouldn't end up with that aunt of hers. The lack of interest that Aunt Karen displayed was nothing short of appalling, and I wasn't exactly the most warm-hearted and engaging person in the world. But even I could see that whoever was living in that girl's phone was much more intriguing to her than anything happening in the real world around her, her little niece included.

"I'm glad your grandmother will feel better after Christmas," I offered, not really sure what else to say. "Are you going to celebrate Christmas with a tree and all?"

"Oh yes," Wendy said, dancing around on the gravel drive. "We have a tree in the closet. It's plastic so it doesn't make a mess. Nana says I can put it up after Thanksgiving."

"That sounds nice. Do you know how to put it up though?"

"I put it up last year. It took me all afternoon. It wasn't hard —just a lot of branches to stick on. I have a horse Christmas ornament. He's chestnut like Personal Best." She paused to watch the yearlings in the pasture by the driveway; they were playing in a big herd of kicking hooves and snapping teeth. "I need one that's dark bay like Christmas," she went on.

Yikes, she was still thinking about that filly we'd sent to Jackson's. *Don't ask about her,* I thought. "We have a nice dark bay—a couple of them. Next time you come I'll introduce you to Tiger. He's in one of the paddocks behind the training barn today."

"How is Christmas? Have you heard about her?"

I hesitated just a moment. "She's fine," I said lightly. "Haven't heard of any problems." That much was true.

"Does her new trainer like her?"

"Loves her." I kicked a stone and shied a rabbit from a patch of high grass in the pasture. "Look, a bunny!"

"Is he going to race her?"

"I don't know."

"I want to go down and see her race. Do you think we could do that?"

"I don't know."

Wendy was quiet for a few minutes. We were nearly to the house when a little red Kia appeared in the drive. "There's your aunt," I said helpfully.

"Yup."

"It was nice riding with you today."

Wendy stopped suddenly and smiled up at me. "Thank you *so* much!" she announced and gave me a bear hug. I squeezed her back, feeling a great blossoming of happiness within. I wanted to *keep* her. I wanted to buy her a pony and feed her ice cream sundaes.

Where had this kid come from? She made me feel like a million dollars—at least when I wasn't feeling guilty for lying about that horse she liked so much. "Come back really soon, okay?" I asked, and I meant it.

"Next weekend?"

I nodded and smiled. "Definitely."

Wendy ran for the car. Then she stopped, just before she opened the passenger door. Her aunt sighed and glowered at her. "You can tell me how Christmas is doing next time," she called, and then ducked into the car.

Great.

Chapter Nine

FIRST THING THE NEXT morning, I took Tiger out for a spin on the track. It was chilly and foggy, with dewdrops clinging to the hairs on my arm and soaking my shirt as we galloped through the blowing clouds. The occasional streetlights posted along the track morphed into strange orange spheres that lit up the fog around them, just enough to tell us we weren't going to run into the rail. Tiger loved it, dragging his head down against the bit so that he could try to pull me around the track. I had my feet out in front of me, standing nearly straight up, using all of my body to hold him back, but it only encouraged him. Tiger was a typical older horse: he knew all the tricks and he used them for fun. He didn't want to get me off his back, he just wanted to get me off his mouth so he could run as fast and far as he liked.

I let him go as we came around the final turn, if only to give my arms a break; I was starting to feel like my shoulders were being wrenched from their sockets. But as soon as I leaned over his neck, planting my hands a little above his withers to balance myself, I knew he'd been pulling so hard because he felt that I wanted to run, too. And he was right—Tiger knew me best.

It *had* been a while; I didn't gallop much anymore, preferring to watch from horseback alongside the track while the exercise riders put the horses through their paces for me. But ever since I'd watched Wendy drive off with her aunt yesterday, I'd felt restless, like I wasn't doing enough somehow. All the business of running the farm, of training from the back of my pony, were ultimately not why I was in the racehorse business. Wendy reminded me, with her boundless enthusiasm and incredible joy in the saddle, that my passion was out here on the track, on the back of a fast horse, two minds set on one goal.

And so I needed this: the wind in my face, causing my eyes to tear; the cold mist in my face, the hot horse churning beneath me. We flew down the stretch hard on the rail and I listened to his hooves drumming and his breath coming loud and fast before I finally stood in the stirrups and slowly asked him to pull up.

We were halfway around the first turn again before his canter strides slowed to his long smooth trot, and I turned him back towards the gap and sat down, asking for a walk so that I could drop my feet from the stirrups and relax. I was breathing hard; so was he: neither of us were in the best shape. His time off while I was in Saratoga had not translated into better, stronger works once we started up again in September, and I had been going extremely easy on him, afraid I might be seeing the end of his racehorse days. Tiger was a gelding and there would be no spot in the stallion barn for him; I didn't think he'd like being a pony and we didn't need another one, anyway, but I didn't want to think about finding a new home for him. I wasn't ready yet.

So instead I thought about Christmas. Tiger settled into his long-strided, ambling walk, nodding his head and flopping his ears, and I retreated into myself to worry about this horse that hadn't meant a thing to me a week ago. Christmasfordee, her grandmother calls her Dee, it's almost Christmas—what were the chances, honestly? And that eerie way the filly had zeroed in on her, focusing her white-rimmed eyes that probably never stayed very long on any one thing, watching the girl as if she had the face the filly had been waiting for her entire life...it was odd, that was all. Very odd.

Wendy definitely had a magnetic effect on certain horses: Personal Best had been enamored with her, of course, and she'd made the opposite impression on Luna—although Luna was a pretty choosy filly in her own way. The more fit she became, the most snooty her attitude, not that she backed it up by running any bullets in the morning. When Wendy had visited yesterday, no one in the training barn had seemed particularly overwhelmed by the kid's presence, whether for good or for ill. What she had with Personal Best, and with Christmasfordee, was definitely a rare thing.

But that didn't mean she was somehow entitled to the horse, I reminded myself, turning Tiger's head inward, towards the inner rail, to back him off before we rode out through the gap and onto the path back to the barn. An emotional connection meant nothing in this world. The filly was a racehorse, however an unimpressive one, and in all likelihood after her retirement she would become a broodmare, if only because Joey really liked her. She'd spend her life in pastures with her foals, who hopefully would not be as lackluster and poorly-built as she was, although the chances of that were slim, and Wendy would go on riding school horses, learning to jump, helping out with barn chores at her hunter barn in exchange for extra riding lessons and show fees, until someday she either gave it all up or went professional. I suspected she'd choose the latter course. She seemed too intense to be a casual rider, although that could just be par for the course for a girl of her age.

But either way, she was going to have to forget about Christmasfordee, chalk it up to a funny coincidence of names of horses she had once known, and embrace the dozens (or hundreds, or thousands) of future horses she would come to know throughout her life.

And one or two of them, with any luck, would have the same emotional connection that she had found with Personal Best and Christmas. I ran my hand down Tiger's hot neck. Every now and then, you find a horse you just love, and who absolutely loves you back.

Tiger snorted.

And one who reads your mind, I thought wryly.

We came back into the training barn, a glowing halo of light surrounding its bustling early-morning atmosphere. The riders had arrived and were mounting up their first set; Alexander was sitting in the saddle on Betsy, who flopped her ears and nodded her head in greeting as we rode down the shed-row. He raised his eyebrows as I approached. "I was wondering what made you leave the house so early this morning."

"I want to get him into a race at Tampa," I explained. "We just ran a really nice half-mile and he isn't blowing too hard."

Alexander nodded. "One more try," he said, a hint of warning in his voice, and I pressed my lips together and nodded back.

In the stall, I accepted the help of the groom who came to hold the reins while I dismounted, then let him halter Tiger while I stripped the saddle and bridle. I dipped the foamy bit in the water bucket as I exited the stall, then turned back to look him over one last time. The groom turned him in a circle, waiting for me to move, yet I lingered, watching Tiger's body, his motion. He was moving evenly, perfectly sound. There was nothing to see. But I watched him for a moment because he was mine, and I loved him, and I worried for him...incessantly.

I felt bad for Wendy then. Because I suspected Christmasfordee was hers, and she loved her, and she was worrying about her. But emotions had no place in this game, and no one was going to give her a four-year-old racehorse, however imperfect, just because she had a hold on her heart.

Chapter Ten

THE GOETHE WAS ONE of those little known Florida hideaways—a massive wilderness of pine and hardwood forest tucked away between the swampy shore of the Gulf of Mexico and the green hills of Ocala. Its sandy trails were a favorite of trail and endurance riders, and I'd even come across drivers, sitting behind their teams of harness horses in specially-made off-road carriages, complete with fat dune-buggy tires to deal with the deep, white-sand footing.

I didn't trail ride much, because who had the time? Recreational riding was a thing of the past in my life. But Alexander suggested it as a Thanksgiving treat for Wendy. After riding with me nearly every afternoon for the past few weeks, she was more than capable of sitting in a western saddle while the sure-footed Betsy picked her way along the well-marked trails, and even if one of the horses spooked at a sudden appearance by a deer or another horse, it was unlikely Betsy would bounce terribly hard and unseat the kid. Betsy was as steady as they came. Plus my pony, Parker, having come from the streets of New York, had figured out that the bunnies and lizards of country living were not going to kill him, either —he was about as bomb-proof as they came.

And Alexander was right—Wendy deserved a holiday treat. Her grandmother hadn't left the couch in a week, she'd reported a few days before. "Her medicine makes her sick," she kept explaining, and I kept nodding my head and saying I was sure she'd feel better really soon. Wendy said she wasn't going to starve or anything; she knew how to make macaroni and cheese and grilled cheese sandwiches, and her aunt was checking on her everyday and bringing her home for supper if she wanted. But it seemed too dreary for words, even for a holiday that I didn't really bother celebrating, to be contemplating whether one was going to have mac and cheese or a grilled cheese sandwich for Thanksgiving dinner. For the first time ever, I wished that I had planned a Thanksgiving dinner of our own, so that I could have invited her over.

But of course there was the fact that Alexander didn't celebrate Thanksgiving and liked to make jokes about colonials when anyone suggested it, and the separate but no less important fact that I cooked about as competently as Wendy. I'd already told our chef, who cooked for us once a week and left us a freezer full of goodies to stop us from ordering pizza every night, not to bother with any holiday dishes.

So the Goethe and a trail ride it was. I asked Wendy the day before Thanksgiving if she'd like to come with me on Friday afternoon, as a holiday weekend treat.

"With the horses in the trailer?" Wendy asked, eyes wide. She was mounted on Betsy with a seat like a princess; I marveled, once again, at how naturally perfect her posture was.

"Yup," I confirmed with a nod. "We'll drive them out there, put their saddles on, and go ride in the woods for a few hours. It'll be a nice break for them."

"Betsy *is* bored with just going around the racetrack," Wendy said. She patted the mare's neck. "She'd love to go out in the woods."

"And so would you, I bet."

"I sure would!" Wendy's face lit up with that incandescent glow I loved.

"It's a date, then." I gave Parker a rub under his mane and the little Thoroughbred shook his head and neck, as if I had tickled him. "Want to try a jog again?"

Wendy's face instantly grew more serious. She was trying to learn to ride Betsy's rather airy trot without bouncing, and though I knew she was going home aching and bruised after every ride, there was no stopping her. "Let's do it," she said in tones of steel, and gathered up her reins.

"Three...two...one!" I chirruped to Parker and off we went, jogging down the racetrack and into the sunset, Wendy grimly trying to sit the trot with a face like a soldier going into battle. I was so proud of her my heart seemed to swell up in my chest, and it was hard to believe that a month ago I had been cursing at the telephone after Linda had demanded I allow the girl into my life.

"Why are all the pine trees in straight rows?"

"That's funny, isn't it?"

We were riding through the pine forest on a perfect fall day. Okay, it wasn't a perfect fall day anywhere but in my imagination. It was about eighty-four degrees and sunny, and the horses were sweating through their skimpy winter coats as if they were in a sauna wearing ermine from head to hoof. But I got cold if the temperature dropped below seventy-two degrees, so I was enjoying the warmth.

And Wendy was right, the pine trees *were* all in straight rows. Towering, skinny, lined up in perfect rows that marched over the sandy hills, the trees already looked like the telephone poles they would probably all end up as one day. Every once in a while we passed through a clearing where the trees had been harvested; seedlings were sprouting through the ground-brush and palmettos, and once or twice a deer had blinked at us from the patchy grass before darting away for deeper cover. Above us, the yellow autumn sun was shining through the bushy tops of the trees, and the pattern of light on the white sand trail were zebra stripes that flashed against my eyelids when I closed them against the glare.

Once in a while the path would angle out of the deep woods and alongside properties that backed up to the woods. We weren't in a rich or desirable part of Florida; these were sandy fields that didn't support much, maybe a horse or a cow per acre if the pasture was fertilized. We were far from cities or towns, as well, so there weren't any commuters building McMansions out here. There was a simple reason, I figured, why this section of Florida was called the Nature Coast: no one wanted to live out here, where the shorelines were swampy, the interior sections were dry and drab, and the closest grocery store was more than an hour away.

We were coming up on one of the lonely hamlets that lined the forest now: I could see a clearing on the left, and sunlight glinting on barbed wire. As we drew nearer the horses lifted their heads higher, pricking their ears. "There's a horse or two up here," I warned Wendy. "Sit deep and put your heels down in case anybody gets silly."

Wendy nodded and did just that, lengthening her legs and settling her heels a little ahead of her knees, so that she had a firm base of support in case Betsy did anything unexpected, like whirl or shy sideways. Sometimes horses seemed more spooked by the sight of strange horses than strange animals.

We drew even with the edge of the sloping pasture. Above it on the hill-top I saw the usual sprawl of rotting wooden buildings, tangled barbed wire, and rusting vehicles pulled up around a single-wide mobile home that had seen better days. The field itself was a rectangle of about two acres, lined on either side by the dangerous wire, with a big sandy patch near the front gate where a rusting water trough and a similarly dying gate had been placed. The grass in the rest of the pasture was thin and scruffy, but what was most interesting was the deep oval that had been worn around the fence line, as if someone just rode around and around and around in endless circles.

As if they thought it was some sort of racetrack.

A horse, standing near the upper-right corner of the pasture, turned from what was apparently a deep contemplation of the rotting barn, a cypress structure half-fallen and tangled with ivy, and regarded our horses with astonishment. The horse's dark coat was dappled golden by the slanting sunlight, and I could just see the white stripe on its face, crowned with a splotch of white star. The horse's body was narrow and its legs long—not your typical ranch horse, but a Thoroughbred. That wasn't so unusual, though: the ranches and mini-farms all around Ocala were dotted with the cast-offs of the racing industry. Everyone within sixty miles of Marion County had a Thoroughbred, I often thought, and it was usually one they'd gotten for free.

The horse turned its head back towards the barn for a moment, ears pricked, as if it had heard a sound inside. I saw the large ears, the coarse profile, that funny big nose, and caught my breath. But I was being foolish. Plenty of horses had that half-dished, half-Roman face. Even Thoroughbreds.

The horse suddenly decided it wanted to see what we were up to, and bolted right for us with surprising power, rocketing down the slope of the pasture. I was astonished by the horse's acceleration and length of stride, and really hoped it had the eyesight and brains and turning power to match; if the horse hit the barbed wire fence that separated its field from our trail, we were going to see some serious carnage. I didn't feel prepared for anything so horrible, and I knew Wendy didn't. Speaking of Wendy—I reached over and put a hand on Betsy's rein, just in case. Wendy, sitting very deep in the saddle, gave me a nervous smile.

"You'll be fine," I reassured her, lifting my left hand to tighten the reins as Parker began to bounce a little bit, watching the approaching Thoroughbred with some concern. Those legs were hammering the ground like pistons, those eyes were wide and white-rimmed, that horse was...*no way*—

"That's Christmas!"

Wendy was out of the saddle before I could say a thing, slithering down from Betsy, who sidled away nervously, nearly jerking her reins out of my hand. Wendy ran in front of Parker and over to the fence line, shoving through the palmettos that had grown up along the trail. *"Whoa, Christmas! Whoa girl!"*

And to my disbelief, that wide-eyed, wild horse actually slid to a halt directly in front of Wendy, her red-lined nostrils reaching out to touch the girl's outstretched hand, her heaving sides trembling as she blew at the girl's familiar scent. I steadied Parker with my left hand and Betsy with my right hand and tried to wrap my head around what was going on, but this was really *too* insane for me. I didn't have a clue.

Wendy, though, seemed to take it all for granted. With one hand rubbing the now-quiet filly between the eyes, she turned and faced me with an accusing glare. "What is Christmas doing *here?* You said she was at the racetrack with a friend of yours! This place is a dump—no horse should live here!"

I didn't know what to say. That the lives of horses are capricious and unpredictable? That every horse was always in danger of ending up in some sandy backyard with the company of broken farm implements and rusty wire fencing? That it was no one's fault and most emphatically not *mine?*

None of that, because there was some guy coming out of the mobile home and I was pretty sure the long thing in his hands was a shotgun. "Wendy," I said, and then, more urgently: *"Wendy. Come back here."*

But Wendy had turned back to the horse, and the filly was practically trying to climb into her lap, rubbing her face against Wendy's hand, her eyes closed with pleasure. They were soulmates, there was no doubt about it. But I didn't think the redneck marching through the scrubby pasture was going to give a damn. I could practically see the murderous gleam in his eyes from here. This was a possessive guy and he didn't look like he wanted a pair of females getting googly-eyed over the filly in his field.

"Wendy, her owner is coming," I hissed urgently, nudging Parker closer to the fence. *"And he doesn't look friendly."*

"What the hell's goin' on out here!" the man bellowed. He was about halfway across the pasture and close enough for me to see the stains on his t-shirt and the rage in his face—what I could see of his face above the bristling thick beard that spilled onto his chest, lumberjack style. This was a true Florida Cracker, living out in the middle of nowhere because he didn't want nobody in his business, and here we were, all up in his business like a pair of fools.

"Nothing," I called. "We're just trail riding. Pretty horse," I added. "Come on Wendy, time to head back! It's getting dark!"

"Your girl needs to leave my horse alone," the man growled. He came up behind Christmas and slapped the filly hard on the rump. She squealed and took off, shaking her head, ears pinned flat to her head. She skidded to a halt in the corner of the pasture about twenty feet away and stood there with her hindquarters bunched, ready to kick out if she was threatened again.

"Christmas!" Wendy called, and then she turned an angry face at the man. "Why did you hit her? She's a good girl."

"Just who the hell are *you?*" he sneered. "Get your skinny ass back on that mule and get out of here. I don't answer to you Yankees about the way I treat my horses. And that there's a *racehorse.* She don't need no little girls hanging off her. You just git." He jounced his rifle from one elbow to the other.

"We're gitting," I assured him. "Wendy, come get back on this horse this instant."

"We can't leave Christmas here!" she turned angry eyes on me. "This isn't the racetrack! There's hardly even any grass for her!"

"Lady, control your daughter."

"She's not my—Wendy, seriously, you're way out of line here. I'm sorry about Christmas, but this is her owner and he is obviously taking perfectly good care of her. Look how fit she is." And it was true: although dirty as any pasture-boarded horse, and with long toes which needed a farrier's urgent attention, the filly was bursting with muscle. Her chest was much more bulky than when I'd seen her a month ago, and her hindquarters were equally built. Someone had put some time into getting her fit. The worn oval in the pasture was making sense now. Maybe this guy was planning on running her at Tampa, who knew? If he'd figured her out, maybe he'd make a little money. Stranger things happened in horse racing. "Come on. You don't have anything to worry about."

"That's right, missis," the redneck agreed. "I take damn fine care of this horse. This is a *racehorse*. Won me two hundred dollars just the other night."

I looked up. "Two hundred dollars?" No track in the country had purses that low.

"That's right. Fastest horse of the night. Eddie Runyon had some Quarter Horse stud, couldn't catch her to save his damn life. She ran the tar out of him. Next time she's going longer and we'll really give them a show."

I was utterly flummoxed. "Wait, were you barrel racing?"

"*Barrel* racing? *Hell* no! This here's a real racehorse. Don't need no barrels." He eyed me suspiciously, as if he'd said more than he'd meant to. "Y'all better just move along now."

"Come on, Wendy," I repeated, now in a serious hurry to get moving. If this old hillbilly hadn't stopped himself, he might have told me a local secret, and I didn't want him to give out any information he'd regret. The Goethe was not like Ocala, with lots of horse-people up in each other's business all the time. We were just visitors here; these folks lived their own lives. "We have to get going or we'll be out here after dark."

Wendy finally gave in and came back over, taking the reins from me and leading Betsy over to a fallen pine log to mount. She cast a final look at Christmas, still huddling in the corner with her ears carefully trained on her owner, her tail swishing. They did not have a happy partnership, that much was for certain. I wondered how I could lie to Wendy, convince her otherwise. I wished the old redneck would have just *pretended* to be nice to his damn horse. It would have made my life a lot easier.

But he just watched us turn and ride away. As soon as we could, I nudged Parker into a jog, and Betsy followed. The effort of staying secure at the trot would keep Wendy occupied until we were well away from the crazy Cracker and his gun, I figured. I didn't need her asking questions that he'd overhear.

I didn't need him coming after us to keep his information to himself.

Chapter Eleven

"WE CAN STILL TURN back," Kerri suggested, her voice tight. "I don't know if this is your best idea."

"Oh, it's *definitely* in my top ten bad ideas. It's right up there with running away to Ocala to ride racehorses. But we're not turning back."

The dirt road we had been driving down for the past five minutes had given way to what was little more than two sandy tracks with thick weeds bursting up between them, brushing the undercarriage of the truck with rather alarming hissing and thunks. We were way out in the wilds of Levy County, not too far from the Goethe. It was a rural area bordering on wilderness, and its tumbledown wire fences and scrubland hills were a world away from the even fences and manicured pastures we'd left behind in Ocala. This was a scrappier, more wild version of Florida, and its residents had been living on the peninsula much longer than my family, or anyone that I knew.

We were deep in Cracker Country.

"What if this driveway just peters out?" Kerri asked helpfully. "There hasn't been any room to turn around for at least a mile."

"It's not going to peter out. Judd said this was the way, and Judd should know."

Of course, I had to hope and pray Judd had given me perfectly clear, perfectly precise instructions, and there was definitely a possibility that he'd misremembered *which* rusty white mailbox I should turn left at once I'd been driving on County Road 493 for eight miles "or so." Judd was a decent farrier and a nice man, but he'd had his run-ins with drugs and booze, like a few other guys I'd known who made their living underneath horses, and I'd seen him forget which horses were kept where and wait patiently for me at the broodmare barn, while I tapped my feet with impatience down at the training barn, with a shed-row full of racehorses who needed new kicks. His memory had definitely taken a hit from some of his recreational hobbies. And he'd probably been kicked in the head more than once, too.

But he'd seemed pretty certain when I'd asked him where the nearest bush track was. "You want the one up at Salt Springs or the one out in Gilchrist or the one down near Otter Creek?"

"Oh, Judd," I'd said disapprovingly—even though I'd asked because I knew he'd have the answer. "Do you really go to those places?"

"Their horses get shoes, too, you know," he'd said cheerfully, and transferred a few nails from the open carton on his tool-box to his cheek. Nails bristling from the corner of his mouth, he bent back over the hoof of the two-year-old he'd been shoeing. "Aren't you glad they're getting such tender loving care from me?" he'd chuckled around his mouthful.

"Of course I am," I'd said apologetically. "And it's the one near Otter Creek, I guess. This horse was down along the Goethe."

"Tons of horses getting trained in the Goethe," Judd announced through his mouthful of horseshoe nails. "Goethe gallopers. That deep sand makes 'em strong."

"Just tell me where the track is."

"Okay. But listen, don't be too obvious, okay? Not a lot of girls at these things, and none of them have all their teeth and pretty hair like you."

"Got it," I'd said, and taken out my phone to make notes as he described the route.

Now I was starting to worry about more than being the only girl with all my teeth—well, besides Kerri. I was starting to worry this was a road to nowhere. On my left, there was a barbed-wire fence encircling a field with a few dozen long-horn cattle. On the right, a drainage ditch dropped away from the road with alarming proximity to the track my wheels were following. I was starting to sweat.

"If you see a place to turn around, please take it," Kerri said.

"Okay." I was getting just scared enough to give in.

Then the pasture on the left ended in a forest of pine trees—more of the overgrown telephone poles like the ones in the preserve. After about fifty feet of slash pines, the landscape opened up again, and there it was: the bush track.

In a great grassy clearing, just about large enough to hold a decent-sized jumping arena, the scene was set for a night of country fun. About twenty or thirty trucks and trailers of varying descriptions were lined up, like we'd happened upon a secret rodeo. There was a mobile smoker and a big man in an apron leaning over it. A few coolers alongside were propped open to showcase their contents: gleaming cans of Coors Light and Bud, ready to add their influence to the night's festivities. Through the gaps between the trailers, I could see horses walking, their riders sitting with short stirrups in light exercise saddles. Beyond it all, a pasture stretched out to a clump of trees on the horizon: a cypress dome, I thought, belying how far west we'd traveled, towards the distant coast of the Gulf of Mexico. We were really, truly, in the middle of nowhere.

"This is going to be messed up," I said, and Kerri nodded.

I parked the truck as close to the driveway entrance as I could, the better for a quick getaway, and we pulled on our baseball caps like they were disguises. Both of them were given out as advertisements for stallions, and I wondered if any of the horses at this makeshift, illegal racetrack were descended from the high-dollar horses whose names were embroidered on our caps.

The music was pumping from an amplifier as we walked across the grass towards the open space beyond the trailers, where I could only assume the racetrack was. Country music, about God and country, guns and girls, Friday night football games and drinking out of plastic cups. There was a rebel flag flying from the oversized CB antenna of a camouflage-painted pick-up truck. Wait, make that two. This was the secret, real Florida, the one they didn't tell the tourists about.

Hell, I thought, as we came through the forest of trailers and found ourselves gazing at the tight bull-pen of a racetrack, the metal bleachers full of cowboy hats and boots, and the little six-horse starting gate set up at the opposite end of the clearing. This was evidently the secret, real *horse racing* they didn't tell the tourists about.

Or any of us.

There were about thirty horses making their way around the track at various speeds, none of them keeping any of the rules about only trotting "the wrong way" or riding slowly to the outside and speedy to the inside. There wasn't even an inner rail, so when riders got annoyed or cut off by another horse, they could just swing across the grass of the infield.

It was sort of like the bedlam and mayhem of the warm-up ring at a hunter show, when every kid on every pony sort of forgets everything they've ever been told about arena etiquette and there is a general sense of impending doom. You're just waiting for tangles of equine legs and shrieking children. That was what the racetrack here looked like, except that most of the horses seemed to be ridden by jockeys old enough to drive, maybe even buy alcohol.

Most of them.

"Is that a kid?" Kerri whispered, nodding towards a spotted cross-bred with long legs and no tail at all that was trotting along the outside of the track. The rider was a baby-faced little boy with no helmet and a big grin. One of his teeth was missing.

"Oh my God," I said. "He can't be more than thirteen."

"He's sixteen if anyone asks," a voice said from behind us. I turned around, heart in my throat, and was shocked to see a familiar face.

"These aren't quite your type people, are they?" Mary Archer smirked, her tanned face sinking into a thousand deep wrinkles. "No lattes here, honey."

Beside me, I felt Kerri draw back a little. I put my hand on the small of her back to help her stand her ground. She knew the depth of my old enmity with Mary Archer better than anyone; she'd been there when Mary had made it her business to discredit me around the barns at Saratoga even while Mary's destructive training practices had sent one horse after another careening down the claiming ladder. And, unfortunately, she knew that Mary had the ability to unnerve me like few other people. But we weren't going to back down now. Not with Wendy's horse on the line.

And that's what I was starting to call the ungainly bay filly in my mind: *Wendy's horse*. I was tired of seeing one small girl get nothing but the short end of the stick every damn time. Looking up at Mary's malicious smile, I was more determined than ever: I was going to get my hands on that horse, bring her back to Cotswold, and pay her bills myself if I had to, but Wendy wasn't going to face another disappointment—not this time, at least. This was her horse.

But I still wondered why Mary Archer was here. Briefly, I considered espionage: she was following me, she was going to spread gossip about me yet again; but I shook the thoughts away. That was over the top, even for her. Anyway she'd stopped bothering about me once the Saratoga meet had ended and her stable was dissolved, her horses sent around the country to new barns. I didn't even know who she was working for these days. "Didn't know you got kicked out of legal racing," I suggested, going on the offensive in hopes it made her go away.

Mary's lip curled and she pushed a lank lock of graying hair behind her ear. "I'm here scouting, just like you. Better hope we don't have eyes on the same nag. That didn't work so well for you last time."

Last time, when she dropped Luna into a claimer so that her boss's nephew could claim her. And I'd lost the shake that day, but I had the horse now. "Whose barn is she in now?" I asked with satisfaction.

"One win since," Mary smirked. "Lotta good all that fuss did ya."

"Whatever," Kerri said, rather unimaginatively, but she was right. "Let's get moving if we want to catch any races." She nodded her head in the direction of the low metal grandstands behind us. I nodded and followed, giving up the advice to stay out of sight. If Mary Archer could show her ugly mug around here, Kerri and I certainly could.

We clanked up the metal steps in our paddock boots, feeling conspicuous and overly English amidst the sea of cowboy boots and oversized belt buckles, and took our seats at a relatively isolated corner near the top. The lower seats of the grandstand were crowded with good old boys in white Stetsons and camouflage caps, drinking from cans of Bud and red Solo cups. A few men tilted their cowboy hats back to stare at us, but they must have figured that if we knew how to find the place, we were okay to be there, because they went back to their beers and their perusals of the chaos warming up on the little bull-ring track in front of them without much more than a grunt and a wink.

"You'd think they'd be excited to see us," Kerri whispered. "If coming out here to look for talent is a thing, which I didn't know it was, they'd probably just think we were more racing people with deep pockets."

"I don't know how deep Mary Archer's pockets actually are," I pointed out. "Or if it's actually a thing trainers do or it's just *her* thing. If she's our ambassador, they'd probably like to run us out of here. She's probably scammed every single person she ever bought a horse from." Mary could sour a crowd just by showing up. She was incapable of honesty, as far as I could tell.

"First race, five minutes! First race, five minutes!" squawked a hitherto unseen loudspeaker suspended from a pole just behind us, which explained why no one else was sitting in this section of the grandstand. Once I had recovered from the ensuing heart attack, I noticed that most of the horses were clearing the course, and half a dozen small, tightly-muscled horses had been gathered near the rusty little starting gate, evidently bought second or third-hand from an Ocala training track.

"Quarter horses," Kerri guessed.

"Quarter race, anyway." I didn't think there were many breed restrictions on tonight's racing card: there was at least some Appaloosa blood in that little roan horse, who had a sparse dappling of black spots across his round hindquarters. "I think it's just divided by distance."

The horses were loaded with, I had to admit, no more than the usual amount of chaos. The Appaloosa reared as the doors behind him were slammed closed, setting off the horses on either side of him; there was a lot of swearing and shouting as they got straightened out—again, the usual. Finally, everyone seemed to have all four hooves on the ground at the same time and the gates were sprung open with a splendid sense of timing on the part of the amateur starter. The jockeys, who seemed to range in age and height from middle-school to middle-aged and jockey-height to basketball-player-height, sent their mounts forward with elbows and heels and voice and stick, kicking up a cloud of dust in their wake as they went galloping down the little sandy track.

The six horses ran as a tightly-packed bunch down the first straightaway, in front of the grandstand, and I gritted my teeth as they approached the first tight turn as one. A horse near the rear got too close to the horse in front of him, clipping heels; he stayed on his feet but fell far behind. His jockey shouted at him and slapped him with his stick like a crazed person. It was violent behavior that would have gotten a jockey ruled off a sanctioned track; here it seemed to be cause for amusement, sending up guffaws from the crowd.

"Whoop him up Jakey!" someone shouted, and there was a chorus of *"Whoop him up Jakcy!"* as the jockey got the horse galloping after the pack again.

By the time the race was over, one chaotic loop of the bull-ring track, lasting about thirty breathless seconds, one horse had fallen, two had stopped running, and one was obviously lame. Obvious only to me, I supposed—the lame horse was also the winner, and he jogged unwillingly to the half-circle of straw bales that was designated the winner's circle. The jockey hopped off and accepted a beer and slap on the back.

I turned to Kerri, who was watching the proceedings with wide eyes and open mouth. "This is brutal."

She smiled weakly. "Let's just hope she's in the next race so we don't have to see too much more of this."

But Christmas wasn't in the next race, or the one after that. We turned and scoped out the field behind the grandstand where the unraced horses were milling about, and the trailers where a few were tied up, pulling at hay-nets or pawing or napping.

"That could be her," Kerri suggested, pointing to a horse far out in the field. "Dark bay, long legs…"

"Why couldn't the kid have fallen for a horse with four white socks and a full blaze?"

Kerri agreed. "We're going to have to wait until we see her up close, that's all," she sighed, turning away from the warm-up field.

She had better enter a race, I thought, and soon. The sun was starting to sink; November days were short, even in the Sunshine State, and the temperature was dropping as well. I pulled my sleeves down as far as they'd go—elbow length— and shivered a little.

And then, there she was.

The horses circling for the sixth race were next to the grandstand. I looked them over: a motley crew of washed-up Thoroughbreds, mostly, with bumpy legs and suspicious tendons. Despite their condition, most of them had never forgotten what race-day meant, or what they had been born for. Their legs were mashed to hell, but their eyes were bright and their heads were high: this was their element. It made my heart thump a little to see them and wonder how many had tried their hearts out on the tracks I knew and ran my horses on. How many had been poised for greatness before an injury or a bad race had sent them off the rails and into the swamps, how many had been retired to a quieter, safer life before they found themselves sold to one of these bush-racers? But if the track was tiny and their bodies were sore, the horses themselves had forgotten it amidst the excitement and anticipation of being allowed to run.

And Wendy's horse was no different from the others, at least not in head carriage and high action. She looked like a little warhorse down there, with her nostrils flared and her eyes ringed with white, her head snapping this way and that as she took in her rivals, the shouting crowd, the sandy track just beyond. She was ready, ready, ready—every sinew and nerve and muscle in her body was electrified, quivering, prepared to go into battle and emerge the victor. She looked good, too, despite being a little light in flesh, despite being rather coarsely groomed. Her muscles were toned and bursting through her skin, a result of galloping up and down that sloping pasture, no doubt. The hill-work had paid off: I actually thought she might be able to pull it off.

"She looks good," Kerri said, echoing my thoughts. And then: "Uh-oh." She nodded her head to a knot of people standing just beyond the circling racehorses.

I looked and saw him standing there, the large bearded bear of a redneck who had chased us away from his property with his shotgun over his shoulder. And of course who was he talking to, but Mary Archer.

Chapter Twelve

"NO NO NO NO no no—" Kerri grabbed the back of my shirt as I started to bound down the grandstand.

"What are you doing?" she hissed. "You can't go down there. What are you going to do—fight her?"

"She's *buying* Wendy's horse—"

"Um, I don't think she is." Kerri pointed. "You have to stay for the whole show."

I leaned over the railing of the grandstand. Kerri was right. The owner had folded his arms across his barrel—no easy feat considering the size of his gut—and Mary was gesturing with her hands, waving her arms, looking generally insane. "Holy crap," I said. "He's refusing to sell."

"It's a Christmas miracle," Kerri said dryly.

"Not quite. If he's refusing to sell to Mary, will he refuse to sell to us?"

"Maybe he just knows Mary's a crap trainer?" Kerri suggested hopefully. "Maybe she finally scammed the wrong cowboy?"

I sighed and sat back down, still keeping my eyes on the pair. But it looked like the conversation was over; Mary was stalking away, shaking her head. A few of the other men in the group were looking after her and laughing. "Maybe you're right." It seemed possible, judging by the way everyone was apparently joking about her. "Maybe no one here will have anything to do with her."

We watched Mary heading across the field towards the parking area. "She's leaving!" Kerri gave me an elbow in the ribs. "They hate her! They won't sell her anything. You have to be pretty awful to not be able to buy off one of these guys."

"She's definitely awful."

The loudspeaker behind us made a preemptive popping noise and we both had time to clap our hands over our ears before it called the horses for the sixth race to the starting gate. I felt my mouth go dry and my stomach lurch. This was it. This was the filly's race—what if she got hurt? What if she won? Either way, I would have to go down and deal with her owner. I didn't look forward to talking to him again, even though this time he wouldn't be armed and I would have a checkbook.

At least, I didn't think he was armed.

I watched him lead the filly over to the starting gate, the kid on her back swinging his legs free of the stirrups and laughing at some joke with him—probably about Mary Archer. Then he turned her over to the guys acting as starters and came back to the grandstand to sit with some friends. He cracked open a beer someone offered him and laughed at another joke, the picture of relaxation.

Meanwhile, I thought I was going to throw up.

Everyone loaded in the gate like the old professionals that they were. Again, it struck me how different this field of horses was from the ones in the earlier races. The Quarter Horses and Appaloosas, the Paints and the crossbreds, they hadn't been racehorses in the legal sense of the word, just horses these guys liked to race. This group of Thoroughbreds, though, took things much more seriously. They knew their job. They lived for their job. They were going to do their job or die trying.

That was the frightening part.

I had my eyes closed when the horses broke from the gate. Kerri grabbed my arm and held on tight, my skin turning white under her fingers. "She's on top!" she hissed in a panic. "She's in front by two!"

I opened my eyes just as the horses sped past us on the way to that horrendous tight turn. Kerri was right—Wendy's horse *had* put her dark head in front and was pulling away from the pack. But she wasn't going to be able to maintain her speed; she was charging into the turn and at that pace, she'd never be able to make the corner.

At the last moment, her jockey nearly stood straight up, his stirrups way out in front of her shoulders as he water-skied her around the turn, yanking back hard on her mouth and then hauling her to the left through his own will and strength. She flung her head up, mouth gaping against the bit, but the gambit worked: she only overshot the turn by a little, running all alone in the center of the track as she made for the backstretch.

"Oh my God," I moaned. "How many times are they going to go around this track?"

"Maybe just once? No one else went further than a quarter mile."

"No one else had Thoroughbreds," I said grimly, and Kerri was quiet.

The answer was three times: they went around the little loop three awful times, coming up on their own tracks so many times that the horses were enveloped in a cloud of dust by the final straightaway. After running wildly all across the track in her bid to stay in front *and* make the impossible turns, the filly was flattening out now, her steps coming without conviction, her body laboring. But she had done it—she had stayed ahead, and before my eyes the winless maiden from Gulfstream won her first race: about six furlongs over white scrub sand, somewhere near Otter Creek, Florida.

"He's not going to sell her now," I said bleakly, watching the owner jump up and give the roaring crowd a good fist-pump.

"He might if he thinks you'll pay a lot for a winner," Kerri suggested.

"Maybe."

"Want to go talk to him?"

"In a minute, in a minute." I had to think what to say. I had to be ready. And I wasn't—not a little bit.

In the end, we decided to tail him back to the horse trailer, hoping that we'd catch him alone. Little by little the crowd of friends around him dissipated; there was another race or two for them to catch, a few more beers to finish, and for all I knew they'd end the night with a hog roast or a fish fry or a hoe-down or something. By the time he reached his trailer, a shiny aluminum gooseneck that was much nicer than anything else I'd seen at his property, the filly's owner was alone, just as I'd been hoping.

He tied her lead-rope to a slat on the side of the trailer and started to uncinch her saddle. Kerri gave me a shove and I stumbled forward. He took one look at me and stopped what he was doing. "What the hell you doin' here?"

"Hi—that was a nice win you had there," I stuttered. How do you come back with that kind of a greeting?

"Huh." He grunted and went back to untacking the horse. "You with that Archer woman?"

"No—God no." I couldn't help it. Just the thought—*ugh*. "I'm not associated with her."

"She thought she was goin' to get some kinda bargain," he said with satisfaction, pulling the saddle off and putting it over the side of the pick-up truck. "She must think we are some dumb folk."

"She thinks everyone is dumb. She has no respect for anyone." Why not.

"And what about you?"

"Me?"

"You think we're dumb?" He put an arm across the filly's withers and leaned on her. She fluttered her nostrils, too tired to be bothered. I longed to take her for a nice walk, give her a good shower and a liniment bath, do up her legs in bandages for the night and give her a hay-net of alfalfa and timothy. The sort of treatment she'd been accustomed to in south Florida, and that she more than deserved after the brave race she had run tonight.

"Not at all. But I do have something to talk to you about," I rushed ahead with my words. "I have a client who is *very* interested in this filly; I'm prepared to offer you a good price for her."

He smirked. "What price?"

"Name it," I countered. I had no idea what a good price was out here.

He pretended to think for a moment, putting one hand up to his forehead and tapping at it. "Think," he muttered. "Think think think. Oh! I have it!" He smiled beatifically at me.

"Go on."

"She's not for sale," he said bluntly, and went back to work, pulling off her bridle roughly.

I swallowed and tried to get my heart out of my boots. "Sir, I'm prepared to pay—"

"Not for sale!" he interrupted, swinging the bridle dangerously. "You Yanks think you can just buy anything you want, don't you? Get the hell out of here! You think I don't know what this horse is? Go back to your damned auctions and your million-dollar studs and leave us alone."

I backed away, my eyes on the snaffle bit at the end of that swinging bridle. I didn't think he'd be above hitting a woman, that much was for certain. He'd already pulled a gun on me. "Sir," I tried, desperate for one last attempt. "Sir, can I just leave you my card, and if you *ever* change your mind—"

"Get out of here!" he bellowed, and the filly spooked, pulling back against her lead. "No more of you people at our tracks! By God, the next Yank out here is gettin' shot, I swear it!"

"Tell 'em, Trav!" someone shouted, and then there were more men showing up from behind the trailer, teeth white in the dusk as they laughed at us. "Get out of here, go on Yankee, go home!"

I grabbed Kerri's arm and we ran, not caring how foolish we looked, just certain that if we didn't get the hell out of there very, very quickly, we were going to end up on the ten o'clock news. And not tonight's broadcast, either. It would take the dogs and the mounted posse a couple of days to find our bodies.

We were slamming around the truck cab as I drove entirely too quickly down the rutted old path, in a rush to get back to civilization. And it was only when we were back on paved road and putting miles between us and the bush track that Kerri asked, "What are you going to do next?"

I turned on the radio. A Christmas carol came wavering through the speakers, from a tower somewhere out in these forsaken sandy hills. *All I Want For Christmas Is You.*

I switched it to NPR.

I didn't have a plan, and I didn't need any reminding of it.

Chapter Thirteen

WENDY WAS GETTING PRETTY good at the posting trot. I watched her make her away around the training track all alone, alternating between rising with Betsy's stride or trying to sit to it. It was a long hard struggle, but we all had to learn how to post and how to sit that bouncy gait. Once you had it, you had it—until you got on a horse with a completely different stride, of course. We'd cross that bridge when we came to it. If there was one thing I didn't see in Wendy's future, it was a horse of her own.

And that was a disappointment I took to heart. I rubbed Parker's neck, slipping my hand into the warmth beneath his neck; it was a chilly day, December starting to make its presence known in north Florida. Between the cold weather and the incident at the bush track, I was feeling fairly low this afternoon. It was amazing how just a few hours could bring about such turmoil in your life, such emotional upset and worry.

When this whole thing with Wendy had started, I hadn't expected to get involved at all. She could come to the races that one day, and that was it. Then it was up to the Rodeo Queens to make sure she learned to ride, and she could figure out getting a horse of her own the way other determined kids with a passion and not much in their pockets always did—if it meant working for someone after school and on weekends, indenturing herself out...well, that was how it was done.

But then this whole thing with this filly had come along and...I couldn't get the idea out of my head. That somehow, Christmasfordee had been Wendy's Christmas present in truth. That the ungainly filly was somehow her destiny, and that Wendy was the filly's destiny. That they could save each other.

Because I knew, as surely as I knew Wendy's life would continue to be hard—even if her grandmother felt better after the holidays, even if her aunt looked up from her phone for thirty seconds to notice her little niece in the room, even if she learned to ride from a proper trainer—that by the same token, the filly was going to have a hard life as well. She might have displayed heart and surprising speed at the bush track, but all the conditioning in the world wasn't going to save her from simply being built to fail. She didn't have the conformation to run hard and hold up. She *shouldn't* be racing and she *shouldn't* be bred, which was another tick in the Wendy column.

Plus, racing on those tracks, with those bull-ring proportions, those tight turns, that terrible footing? I shook my head. "No," I said aloud, and Parker's ears flipped back to listen. But I didn't have anything else to say. She ought to be Wendy's horse, and I was horribly frustrated that she couldn't be. That was the beginning and end of the conversation. Where else could it turn?

Horse and rider were coming back around the turn. The weak winter afternoon light shone down from the deep blue sky, accenting the oaks turning brown along the rail, Betsy's fuzzy ears which pricked as she zeroed in on Parker waiting in the gap, Wendy's face red with exertion as she huffed and puffed her way through another ten strides of posting trot. "Good job!" I shouted. "You can walk now!"

She pulled up Betsy with obvious relief and they came walking over to join us at the gap. "That was hard," she panted.

"You did so good," I told her. "You're almost ready to canter by yourself." She'd only cantered right next to me, on the leading rein. But I figured she'd been riding for more than a month now, so I was probably being too cautious. "Next time," I promised.

Wendy smiled that brilliant smile of hers.

Back at the barn, rubbing the sweat from the shaggy ponies with towels, Wendy asked me what I was doing for Christmas. I thought. "Not much," I admitted. "We were going to go the Keys for a few days, but we have runners the week beforehand and I don't know how many times I can drive to south Florida in a month. I'll be glad to move the horses back here when Tampa opens. What about you?"

She shrugged and rubbed Betsy's neck with the towel. "Nothing really. My aunt is going to Pensacola to be with her mom. My Nana said she'll order us something for dinner and we can watch a movie."

I swallowed over the lump that was rising up in my throat. "That sound since. Do you have a favorite Christmas movie?"

"I like Harry Potter," Wendy admitted. "And *The Little Mermaid.*"

"Me too," I said. "You should watch both of those. And think of me when you're doing it."

"I will," Wendy vowed. "I think of you every single day."

When I came inside that evening, Alexander was flipping through the racing news on his iPad. "Alex?" he called as I was standing in the mud-room, pulling off my boots. "I saw something you'll find interesting."

"Oh yeah?" I came into the living room and leaned over the back of the couch, planting a kiss on his cheek. "I had the most wretched afternoon. Poor Wendy. I can't even stand it anymore."

"Did she fall off?" He was pulling up a website. "It happens."

"No, it's just her entire *life*. I can't stand her life."

He put a hand on my hair. "You're doing a good job brightening it up. I'm sure she appreciates you."

I remembered her words, the seriousness in her face: *I think of you every day.* "I wish I could do more."

"Look—" he put the tablet in my hand and pointed at its glowing face.

I gasped.

"Linda, listen—"

"We don't have the funds to keep a horse for someone, Alex, I'm sorry." Linda smiled apologetically and tightened her grip on her red Starbucks cup. "We provide a one-time-only commitment. In this case it's riding lessons for a year. How much would it cost to pay for the life of a horse in one installment? That's an impossible request."

A sprightly rendition of *Sleigh Ride* started up over the cafe speakers, which I thought just added to my argument. "Linda," I began patiently, which is not the most common way for me to speak to humans, "I am going to take ownership of the horse. That way there's no question about who is paying her bills. But I want her *for* Wendy. She'll get six months off and then we'll have someone help Wendy learn to train her. She won't do the hard stuff, but she'll help. And in a year or two she'll be ready to show and she'll have a great horse to do it on. *Her* horse." I didn't bother adding in the existential stuff about the horse obviously falling under Wendy's spell or anything. I wanted my case to make sense from a rational point of view.

And it was starting to work. Linda was quiet, considering. She took a sip from her cup, massive tacky rings flashing under the LED lights of the Christmas tree next to our table.

"It'll be a Christmas present—from all of us. The ultimate Christmas wish."

"This was all supposed to be her Christmas wish," Linda said doubtfully. "The trip to the races, a years' worth of riding lessons. What will people think, that we're going to buy their kids ponies? We can't do that every year. We have a limit of five thousand dollars per wish. It's in our charter."

"Then it will be from me. From Alexander and me. Inspired by the generosity of the Rodeo Queens and a genuine desire to retire a deserving horse in danger."

"You want to word it like that?" Linda arched a plucked eyebrow. "I don't think Bill will like that. She's being run at a sanctioned track now, so surely she isn't as bad as off as you thought."

I sighed into my coffee. Of course her husband, Bill Swanson, was one of the good ol' boys, with his head in the sand, who didn't believe any horse was ever abused or run past the point of safety in horse racing. "Fine. We'll leave that part out. But I can assure you it's true. This filly has no business running. However this guy has her juiced up and running like she did, it's going to be the death of her."

Linda fluttered her eyelashes, doing her delicate Scarlett O'Hara impression. "I'll have to take it to the committee," she said finally.

I put down my empty cup. Overhead, *Sleigh Ride* segued into *Jingle Bells*. Christmas really was all about horses, wasn't it? "I'm claiming the horse the first moment I can." I told her, getting up. "Let me know if you want the Rodeo Queens involved. But either way, I'm getting Christmasfordee."

Chapter Fourteen

"*HOW DO PEOPLE LIVE here? SERIOUSLY HOW DO PEOPLE LIVE HERE?*"

"Alex, please relax. And get your head inside the car. And roll the window up."

"Alexander, this place is the seventh circle of hell and I am going to kill myself if this traffic does not start moving."

"I'm sure there's a traffic accident," Alexander said primly. "We'll get moving again soon."

Not soon enough, I thought, hitting the button to roll the window up. All around me, lanes and lanes of concrete. All around me, rows and rows of unmoving cars, growling in the December heat. The temperature was eighty-six degrees. The palm trees were lifeless and still on an afternoon without a sea breeze. The air was heavy with oil and gasoline. It was a tropical nightmare. It was Christmas in Miami.

"We're not going to get there in time," I chanted nervously. "We're not going to get there. You know who is? Mary Archer is. She's going to get Wendy's horse."

Alexander sighed. "There is no way of knowing that. For all you know, she offered that man three hundred dollars for the horse."

"Hardly! I offered him *whatever he wanted* and he said no way. He didn't turn her down because she low-balled him."

"I didn't *say* that—" Alexander stopped himself. "It will be fine," he said simply, and then he put the car in park.

Why not? We weren't going anywhere.

Just as I'd told Wendy two weeks ago, we hadn't planned on driving to South Florida again after our horses' last races. We'd run Luna and Shearwater the week before. Luna came wilting from a big start to a fourth place finish; Shearwater ran late for second. I was happy for both of them, but ready for them to come home for a while. I hated having them so far from home; at least running at Tampa was relatively nearby. If the Gulfstream season had been lackluster, at least no one had gotten hurt.

But as soon as I'd seen that Christmasfordee had shown up on the works list at Sunshine South, I'd known there was no chance of avoiding Miami for the rest of the racing season. Somehow, that owner of hers had gotten someone with a trainer's license to take her on, and I had no doubt they were going to put her into a claimer as quickly as possible, to strike while the iron was still hot—and the horse was still sound.

And so while the Rodeo Queens debated whether or not they wanted to add their support to the project, I watched the overnights carefully, waiting for her name to be announced. When it finally came out, for a claiming race for maidens at six furlongs at the short Everglades Park meet, I couldn't believe the date: Christmas Day.

"This is all too weird," Kerri said when I showed her, and I had to agree. The Christmasfordee thing was getting stranger every minute. But that just made me more determined to make it happen. There was something here that was meant to be. There was something here that was destiny. And I was going to be the one to see it through.

Alexander, bless him, saw no problem with the scheme. "Thank God she's not running at Gulfstream," he commented after he agreed to the plot. "I'd much rather spend five grand on a pet than twenty."

And I had to agree. The Everglades Park meet had much lower tags—and much cheaper horses to match them. After the race she'd given everyone at the bush track, I thought she actually stood a chance of winning—if she was training the same way she had been a few weeks ago.

"She must have been on the uptick when Joey Armstrong bought her," Alexander had gone on.

"Are you saying you were wrong to kick her out of the barn?" I was only messing around; Alexander would never admit he was wrong.

"Oh, I wouldn't go that far," he said, as usual not disappointing me. "She's still a mess from a conformation point of view. That narrow chest and those spindly legs...no thank you. And the hooves will cost us, too, you know. But she might have been on the verge of finally breaking her maiden, yes."

And so I thought she was today, too. My only hope was that I could get a claim in before she went to post. If she won at Everglades, her owner would never sell—and there was a girl sitting in a trailer in Ocala, watching *The Little Mermaid* with her sick grandmother, who deserved this horse more than anything.

I rolled down the car window again and stuck my head out. "*FOR THE LOVE OF GOD, MOVE! MOVE!*"

❧ ⮞⮞⮞ ⮜⮜⮜ ❧

But it took more than an hour for traffic to start moving. A few minutes after my last outburst, we watched the helicopter from the hospital landing in the distance, and then the police helicopters. "Someone is having a bad day," Alexander commented. I nodded. I wasn't the only one having a crappy Christmas.

When we eventually got moving again, in fits and starts, I had all but given up on getting to Everglades Park in time. The aging old racetrack was far, far on the south side of Miami's sprawl, built out in swamplands on fill dirt dredged up from early drainage canals, and populated mainly by mosquitos when it wasn't in use as a track. I still wasn't sure what the motivation had been for building out here, but Everglades was apparently still a popular Christmas Day attraction for a certain south Florida demographic: mainly the ones who drove rusty old muscle cars, judging by the cars surrounding us. The traffic to get into the facility, located on a two-lane country road, was backed up for miles. I took one look at the endless river of brake-lights and nearly burst into tears.

"What are we going to *do?*" I asked, and Alexander had just shrugged.

"Hope for the best," he said.

It was twenty minutes to post and we were still a mile away in inching traffic when my phone buzzed. I squirmed in my seat and pulled it out. I looked at the screen a moment.

"What's wrong?" Alexander asked.

"It's Linda," I said, puzzled.

"Answer it!"

So I did. "Linda?"

"Alex, where are you?"

"What? I'm in traffic outside Everglades Park...why?"

"Oh! That explains it!" I heard Linda talking to someone else. "How far away are you?"

"I'm at least a mile...I'm never going to make it in time to drop a claim. Why—what's going on?"

"Oh, honey, everyone decided at the last minute we were going to make this a Rodeo Queens-sanctioned event. We came down with a film crew from the news and everything. Did you bring the little girl? Wendy?"

I shook my head in disbelief. "No, she spent the day with her grandmother, and Linda, seriously, I'm not going to get there in time!"

"Oh, I'm sure you will."

"No, there's literally *no* chance!"

"Everything will be fine—oh, I need to go. Call us as soon as you get here!"

And the call ended.

I looked at Alexander in disbelief. "I think she lives on another plane of reality."

He nodded. "They all do."

Everglades Park was decked out in tinsel and holly for the season, and white twinkle lights glistened in a tableau of wicker deer, grazing near the track's vintage sign out front. But I wasn't looking at any of it. Christmas, I was certain, was ruined, and I didn't want anything to do with it now.

The race had just gone off.

No radio station was broadcasting the call, no one on Twitter was live-tweeting it. It was an unimportant five-thousand-dollar maiden claiming race on a holiday not normally associated with gaming and going to the races. Nothing that happened today was important to anyone but the tiny cluster of connections of each horse running, and a few thousand gamblers with money on the horses. And to me, and to Wendy.

Alexander pulled up to the clubhouse entrance and a valet came out to take the keys. We went in, flashing credentials at the bored girl in the ticket-booth, and walked straight past the betting windows and the escalators to the boxes where most patrons would turn, heading instead for the apron near the wire, where we'd be able to see the finish line, and the winner's circle. The horses were galloping out there somewhere, I could hear the caller frantically hurling out names, but it was echoing in the big structure, the words garbled, and I didn't know who was where. I didn't know where they were. Only that they were out there, and that Wendy's filly was one of them, and I hadn't arrived in time to put in my claim.

I didn't waste time looking at the monitors as we passed them, didn't try to see where she was. I just walked as fast as I could, Alexander at my side, holding my hand tightly—so he was nervous too, so this meant something to him too. We burst out of the building and into the hot sun, to join the crowd of people on the apron, the cigarette smoke and beer fumes rising up around us, as the horses went spilling around the final turn and into the homestretch. I stood back and looked at the screen in the infield—of course. There she was. Her bright white star showing as her forelock was blown back by her own breeze, her dark neck slick with white sweat in the unseasonable heat, there she was, Christmasfordee, cruising for home on Christmas Day.

"Oh *there* you are!" I felt a hand on my elbow and turned reluctantly—it was Linda, her Kentucky Derby chapeau a ridiculous overstatement for the provincial track, her white hand sprinkled with gems as if she was a child running loose in a vintage store. She smiled, coral lipstick stretching across her papery cheeks. "I'm glad you made it. Look! Here she comes!" And she pointed—I looked back in time to see Wendy's filly come under the wire, the winner by five lengths. I watched her gallop past us and on towards the clubhouse turn, her jockey standing in the stirrups, and thought, once again: *I'll never get her now.*

"She's beautiful!" Linda sighed. "What a lovely horse!"

"I can't wait to take her home," drawled a familiar voice.

I felt sick to my stomach. "So you got her, Mary?" I said, trying to play nicely.

Alexander put a hand on my shoulder.

Mary slipped up in front of us, smirking in that familiar way. "I was here at nine a.m. You have to allow for traffic in Miami, honey, didn't you know that? Maybe you're more of a country girl than I realized."

"I hope you do well with her," I muttered, looking at the ground. Mary flounced away. I turned to Linda. "Linda, I'm sorry I didn't get here in time. You guys went to all that trouble —" Behind her, I could see a cameraman and a reporter setting up for a shoot with the racetrack in the background. Two of the Rodeo Queens were engaged with their compacts, doing a thorough re-painting of their faces. "What's going on? You're still doing a story?"

The horses were jogging back to the wire now, and I watched a groom walk out to catch Wendy's filly. She was hot and tired, but the groom had a more sympathetic hand than her owner—than her *old* owner—and had a bucket and sponge at the ready to slather her hot face with cool water. Mary was leaning over the fence proprietarily, she was watching the steward do that walk of doom, carrying her red tags to hook on the bridles of claimed horses...a *lot* of red tags, as it happened. I saw Mary lean back, confused.

"Linda?" I asked. "What's going on?"

And Linda just laughed. "Oh honey," she said. "We *all* have credentials, you know. We just figured it would be harder for any other claimer to lose a twelve-way shake than a two-way."

Alexander joined her laughter. "Well played, Rodeo Queen," he chuckled. "Your math is correct."

Chapter Fifteen

KERRI DUSTED HER HANDS off and stepped back to see the results. We'd been working for at least two hours, and now I thought things might actually be done.

"This is gorgeous," Alexander said from behind us. He'd hung up the garland along the front of the training barn with the help of a few grooms and an extension ladder and then spent the rest of the time watching us ladies go nuts with twinkle lights and peppermint sticks. "It looks like Candyland."

I went to stand next to him, leaning back against the bar of the shed row railing. "It *does* look like Candyland," I breathed, and he clapped a hand on my shoulder. Kerri swung her hands and just gazed at it in pleasure.

Christmasfordee had her hay-net tied up inside her stall, filled with plenty of rich alfalfa to keep her from being too tempted to eat the Christmas finery that adorned the stall's front. And it was a good thing: I'd go nuts if that horse messed up our beautiful decorations after all that hard work! The pine garland draped dramatically from the boards at the stall wall's top, with more wrapped around the blanket rack and hung all over with candy canes, the lights blinking all over the entire confection. "*This* is a party," I declared.

"And it's time for the guest of honor," Alexander announced. He slipped my phone out of my back pocket and dangled it in front of me. "Call the princess and tell her that her presence is required at the stables."

⤜⤜⤜ ⤛⤛⤛

I had never been so nervous in my entire life.

"I've never been so nervous in my entire life," I told Kerri, because I felt like I needed to say it out loud.

"I don't see why. It's not like she's going to be *disappointed* you bought her her dream horse and then decorated her stall up to look like a Christmas wonderland."

Kerri was, as usual, making excellent points. "This is why I keep you around."

"Here she comes!" Alexander announced, watching from the barn's central aisle. I retreated into my desk chair and started spinning it in circles. "Alex?" he called. "Come on out, you'll miss it."

I came creeping out of the office, my stomach full of butterflies. And why? Of course she wasn't going to be upset. The only question was if she was going to be *so* excited that she did something awkward, like faint, or throw up.

The aunt got out of the car, her phone in her pocket for once, and went to the passenger side to open that door. That was new. Then Wendy climbed out of the backseat. She looked around, pushing her thin red hair behind one ear as she squinted up at the garland along the eaves of the training barn, and then at Alexander, Kerri, and I, standing in the central area grinning like the cats in the canaries. "Is something going on?" she asked, her childish voice piping. "What's with the decorations? It hasn't been Christmas for almost a week. You only just put stuff up?"

Then she came a little closer, and saw the lights on the stall inside. "What's happening?"

"Come in!" I cried, unable to bear it another second. "Get in here and see!"

Wendy put her hands over her mouth, and then I heard a thin whinny and remembered that the filly would be just as happy to see her girl as Wendy would be to see her. "The game's up," I told Kerri and Alexander. "Christmas is going to be very happy."

"I should say so," Alexander agreed, and we went into the shed-row together to see the happy moment.

It was enough to bring tears to my eyes. The filly was leaning out over her webbing, her head pushed against Wendy's chest. And Wendy had her face pressed close to the filly's, her cheek in the luxurious dark forelock, just whispering.

Just whispering.

We watched for a moment, wiping at tears we didn't want to admit to, and then I heard a rustle behind us. I turned and saw a bent woman pushing at a walker, making her difficult way into the clay of the shed-row. Close at her elbow was Wendy's aunt, the mysterious young woman who never paid any attention to Wendy. Now she was hovering over the woman who could only be Wendy's grandmother, as nervous as a nurse with an overambitious convalescent. The senior woman looked tired and thin, but when she looked up and met my eyes I saw the same steely courage that I saw in Wendy, and I had a surge of hope: maybe she really was going to feel better after the holidays!

She came up next to me and stopped to catch her breath. "So this," she said after a moment. "This is the horse Dee is always going on about."

"Yes," I said, and then admitted it all: "We bought her. We're keeping her for Wendy—for Dee. She'll need some time off and some new training, but hopefully she'll make Dee a nice horse someday. She won't always be a racehorse."

Wendy's grandmother nodded. "That was very kind of you. I can't begin to thank you...so, thank you. I won't worry too much about the racehorse part; it doesn't look like she'll have too much trouble with her. Her parents were racing folk, did you know that?"

"I didn't." It shouldn't come as much surprise; this *was* Ocala, after all.

"They loved horses," the old woman said thoughtfully. "They were on their way to the farm where they worked..." She swiped at her eyes. "They'd be so happy to see Dee learning to ride."

I blinked, my own eyes hot and prickling. We were silent for a moment, watching the girl and her horse.

"Thank you," the grandmother said again.

I put my hand on her thin one and gave it the lightest squeeze. "It's my pleasure," I told her. "Thank you for letting us help."

We were interrupted from what might have been a very extended session of public crying by the approach of the aunt, who still had no phone in sight. "Karen," I said, thankful for the diversion. "Thanks for bringing Wendy over. I know it isn't your favorite thing to do."

Karen actually blushed. "I'm sorry I've been so preoccupied. I had things going on...it's not a problem anymore."

"She had *boy* trouble," Wendy's grandmother hissed in a loud stage-whisper, and Stacy nodded and shrugged, embarrassed.

"Don't worry about it." I turned my attention back to Wendy, who was planting a big smooching kiss right on Christmas's nose. "Look at those two. Smitten with each other."

Wendy looked my way then, and her face had that brilliant incandescence that I loved. She was glowing with joy, standing there amidst the Christmas lights and the candy canes and the evergreen and the horse she loved more than anything. It was late, but Christmas had come at last for Wendy, and for her filly.

I was surprised she could tug herself away from the horse for even a second, but Wendy gave her a last pat before she came up the shed-row, holding herself back from running as she knew was proper in a barn. She smiled up at me tremulously. "You did this," she said.

"I wish I could take all the credit," I smiled. "But a lot of people did this. And I think officially Rosemary Wood signed the ticket." Rosemary was the Rodeo Queen whose claim eventually won out at Everglades Park. The racing officials had been a little taken aback at twelve claims on one five-thousand-dollar runner, but rules were rules. A curly-haired woman had dropped numbered balls into a pill bottle, shook it carefully, and pulled out Rosemary's number.

"I know a lot of people helped," Wendy admitted. She looked around: at her aunt and grandmother, at Alexander and Kerri. "But," she whispered, coming in for a hug, which I knelt to receive, "You *did* it."

I've never liked children very much, never wanted any of my own, never paid much attention to them. Horses were more my thing, and that hadn't changed. But there was no denying the thrill of having a child wrap her arms around my neck, the satisfaction of having made her life more special, the simple happiness that came from making *her* happy. So I hugged her back, bent over in the clay of the shed row, while a Christmas racehorse looked on from a stall turned into Candyland, and our family stood around and cheered for us.

The End

Turning for Home

Ready for the next book in the Alex & Alexander Series? It's time for *Turning for Home,* a critically-acclaimed and award-finalist novel about racehorse retirement. Alex doesn't feel ready to retire her beloved horse Tiger, but he's giving her all the signs. And when she finds herself embroiled in an animal abuse controversy through no fault of her own, Tiger's retirement might be the only way to put the polish back on her tarnished reputation. Explore the divide between racehorses and sport horses, as well as everything they have in common, in *Turning for Home.*

Read the first chapter now!

Turning for Home
Chapter One

"Hey Alex, that horse still running?"

"Stick around, I think he gonna win the last race!"

"Yeah, too bad you entered him in the eighth, huh?"

I smiled congenially to our hecklers and then, with a display of the ladylike elegance I am known for, flipped Eddie and Mikey the finger. The railbirds guffawed and went back to their hard work holding up the backstretch rail. They had the last few races to lose yet.

"Don't listen to them," I told Tiger, who was most manifestly *not* still running, but who was prancing along beside me, every inch The Tiger Prince and seeming to have absolutely no idea that he'd just run forty lengths behind the winner of the bottom-most allowance race Tampa Bay Downs had to offer. "You're just having a bad patch, that's all."

Tiger eyeballed a candy wrapper alongside the horse-path, considered it for a moment, and then gave in to his deepest, naughtiest desires: he snorted at the wrapper and spooked hard. Since the candy wrapper was to his right, that meant he spooked to his left—directly into me. I grunted as his rock-hard shoulder collided with my (much smaller, lighter, weaker) shoulder, then gave him a solid *whack* with the knotted end of the leather lead shank, right on his big handsome hindquarters, knocking sand out of his hide with the impact. "Brat!"

Tiger leapt forward, hit the nose chain and came to a screeching halt, snorted once again, shook his head, and finally subsided, contenting himself by returning to his high-stepping jig. He was the picture of a racehorse in fullest bloom of youth and energy.

He was six years old and sliding downhill fast. Speed had deserted Tiger, and all he had left was hubris. Of *that,* his reserves were endless.

I kicked at a seashell dotting the horse-path and sighed.

The fact was, Eddie and Mikey Tipton, the brother-trainer-wonder-duo who considered themselves the backside comedy troupe, hadn't been calling out any jokes I hadn't heard before. I'd even told that joke more than a few times. When horses run that bad, that's just what racetrack people say, then we shake our heads to one another, once the unlucky trainer is out of earshot, and wonder what they're going to do with that slow-ass horse of theirs. Turn it out, drop it in class, give it away, breed it...well, that last one wasn't an option for Tiger.

The racetrack rail along our left gave way to short-cropped grass as we slowly walked into the stable area. Low green barns ran in tidy rows; horses peered over their stall webbings to see their compatriots returning from the eighth race. A man leaned over the railing of his barn, feed buckets in hand. "Sorry about the race, Alex," he called. "Maybe next time, huh?"

"Thanks, J.T.," I replied, with what I hoped looked like a smile. J.T. was a good guy. He waved, turned back under the stable banner that read *Speed To Burn Racing Stable,* and got on with evening feeding.

We turned into the shed-row of our own barn, Tiger dancing beside me, and Alexander turned from his perusal of some other horse hidden within a stall, some other horse to distract him from ours.

My eyes met his and he smiled ruefully.

"Surprised he's not still running," Alexander said lightly.

I walked on past him without a word.

I just didn't have the joke in me this time.

"Alex?"

I paused and looked back, pulling up Tiger. The horse blew hot air on my wrist and shook his head impatiently. Standing still was not in his post-race agenda, and he knew it. Time to walk the shed-row, pausing for a sip of water every second turn. Time to make faces at that filly at the north corner that hated him so much, she had to bare her teeth and take a chunk out of the wall every time she saw him. Time to spook and rear every time he passed the Monster in the Muck Pit, just like nearly every other horse in the barn. "What? I have a hot horse here."

Alexander spread his hands in a consoling gesture that just looked helpless instead. But his blue eyes were kind, which I appreciated—I would have expected at least *some* impatience from Mr. Never Forget This Is A Business. Empathy would be a welcome improvement. "Look—I know it was bad. But no one is talking about it. At least you have that. Did you hear about those horses in the Everglades?"

Oh Lord, yes. I nodded stiffly; it wasn't a story I felt up to talking about right now. I'd been in the paddock, saddling Tiger for his race, when the Everglades story broke. An outrider scrolling on his phone while waiting for the post parade had found some headline on Twitter—three horses, three *Thoroughbreds*, had been found abandoned and starving, wandering somewhere in the Everglades, in a piney upland, I figured, where a little bit of grass would push through the sand. Most of the non-natives were busy asking how a horse could be wandering around in a swamp for any length of time. The Everglades were way more than water and alligators. Not that it mattered. This was going to be a major scandal, and bad for all of us in the racing game. As it should be. Until the rotten apples were sorted out, most of America seemed content to throw out the whole bushel—Alexander and I included. Maybe, at least, they could prosecute this particular apple. "Any more news on it? Whose horses they were, maybe? They have to find whoever dumped them and throw the book at them."

"None. But I just wanted you to know—*that's* the gossip all over the track. If you were going to throw a clunker, this was the race to do it in. No one's going to be talking about you tonight."

"Thanks," I sighed, and clucked to Tiger to walk on. He squealed and danced next to me, his hooves throwing up a cloud of dust to glitter in the golden light of late afternoon. "I don't even know why I'm walking you out," I told him. "I don't even know how you're hot from that little canter around the track. You big embarrassing dummy. Don't you know I have a name to maintain? How am I going to lift my head around here?" But Alexander was right—with a fresh abuse scandal breaking upon the racing community, my worst showing yet from Tampa's winter meet would go unnoticed. That was a mercy, anyway. It hadn't been a wonderful winter so far, not for me.

"I almost wish I was back in Saratoga," I went on, and Tiger jogged beside me, his ears flicking between the shed-row ahead and my familiar voice. We'd been together for how long now? The years went by in a blur of foaling seasons, hot summers, wet autumns, with every morning bringing the same chores. And except for leaving him behind for last summer, when I went racing in Saratoga, we'd spent time together nearly every day. Tiger was more pet than racehorse to Alexander and me, and I was even worse about it than Alexander was.

I galloped Tiger, I saddled Tiger in the paddock, I caught Tiger after the race. I kept Tiger at home with me between races. He'd been an anchor in a dangerous time for me, when my world was stormy and I felt adrift from everything I had ever loved. I had a special place in my heart for my wicked colt, Personal Best, who lived up to his name in every way as the best horse I had ever bred, foaled, and trained; I had a special attachment to my foolish filly Luna Park, who had been on the road to ruin when I claimed her and gave her a re-education.

But when Alexander had proposed that we run our good horses at Gulfstream over the winter, and went so far as to say they ought to be stabled at a South Florida training center for easy access to the track, I'd given the go-ahead. I'd kissed P.B. and Luna good-bye, along with Virtue and Vice and

Shearwater. I'd kept Tiger, though. You couldn't expect me to give up all my pets at once.

Bathed, cooled out, and legs done up in alcohol wraps, Tiger attacked his hay-net with all the viciousness of a real tiger, leaning over the stall webbing and tearing at the green ball of hay with tooth and muscle and temper. I leaned against the rail of the shed-row and watched him. Alexander leaned against the office door and watched me. I ignored him with the pointed air I'd perfected over the years. I didn't want to talk about it.

But as usual, Alexander wanted to define when we'd have the discussion. "You know it's time, Alex."

"It was a bad race."

"It was an embarrassment."

I ground my teeth. Tiger wrenched hay from his net with long yellow teeth. They weren't the teeth of a young horse anymore. Racehorses started their careers with little nubbins, barely grown out of their milk teeth. They left their careers when they were literally long in the tooth...the lucky ones, anyway...

"Can I at least have a cup of coffee before we talk about this?"

"That I can do." Alexander stepped back and waved his arm towards the office door. "Come into my castle, madam."

The office-slash-tack-room was half the size of our big comfortable office in the training barn back at Cotswold, and into that half we'd had to squeeze a saddle rack, heaped with saddle towels and girths and one perfect little exercise saddle, as precious as a child's toy, for the handful of horses we had sent down from Cotswold for the winter race meeting. One corner was occupied by steel trash cans, their lids held down by bungee-cords to discourage crafty raccoons, and a small mountain of feed supplement buckets . My gaze flickered over their familiar labels: joint lubricants, immune boosters, hoof builders, vitamins, electrolytes, even powdered garlic to ward away mosquitoes and biting flies. Our horses got nothing but the best, but I hadn't taken a multi-vitamin since I was a kid.

Wedged into the opposite corner, commanding a small view of the shed-row and the hot-walking machine beyond, was a thrift-store desk, a rusting filing cabinet topped with a dusty coffeemaker, and a small television of impressive vintage. On the floor, a small refrigerator groaned its way through the warm winter afternoon. I opened it now and pulled out a little carton of vanilla creamer. If I was going to have to listen to how badly my horse was racing, I was going to spoil myself with some decadent coffee.

Alexander eyed the creamer but didn't say anything; he didn't believe in spoiling good coffee with flavors and syrups. He set out two mugs with the farm logo on them, chipped and battered, the words *Cotswold Farms* in strong white Roman letters striding across a green field, and when he poured, he supportively left enough room in mine for a healthy dose of creamer.

I practically turned the coffee white as milk.

He looked at me, eyebrows raised.

"I've had a rough afternoon," I explained, and took a long draft of sweet milky indulgence. "You're lucky I'm not demanding an ice cream sundae right now."

Alexander grinned. "That sounds good, actually."

"There's a Friday's right down the street."

"Maybe later. Let's talk about this right now."

"It isn't as if he couldn't have done better in the race." I dove right in, fortifying myself with a gulp of sugar masquerading as coffee. "He's been training perfectly well. He went out there with two excellent works on paper. He was almost the favorite."

Alexander put on a pair of reading glasses, the better to peer at me over the lenses with. They were a rather recent accessory which he enjoyed balancing precariously at the end of his nose for this very purpose. It gave him a fussy, headmaster-ish look, which he loved. It made him feel very wise. I had a feeling he was starting to believe I knew a bit too much for his comfort. He needed to do his wise old owl bit if he was going to continue to feel superior to me, and feeling superior to everyone was part of Alexander's personality. It was one of the things I liked best about him. I wouldn't have him any other way, even if he made me crazy nearly all the time. In the spirit of fairness, of course, I repaid the favor in spades.

"Alex, he ran forty lengths behind the winner," Alexander began in a measured, *let's be reasonable here* sort of tone. "I think that we have discussed this eventuality and come to the only reasonable conclusion."

"I'm just saying he loafed. He wasn't trying. I'm not saying anything else." I didn't actually know what I was saying. It was all nonsense. But I was desperate not to face this. I couldn't run him in a claimer without risking losing him—and he'd shown today that he wasn't going to win at the allowance level. All I really knew was that Tiger was going to have to leave the training barn, and I didn't know where he would go.

Still, I wasn't going to lose him without a fight.

"I wish he hadn't ended with such a bad race," I went on stubbornly. "It's a terrible way to end his career. He was a good solid runner. He deserves a better send-off than that."

Alexander sighed, as Alexander sighed so often. It was his sigh that reminded me I could be a real trial to him, but he loved me anyway, or that he loved me because of it, who knew? He was just as insane as I was, in the end. We were in the racing game, weren't we? Filling our lives with horses, day in and day out? That didn't say much for our good sense. He ran his finger along the rim of his coffee mug, making the cheap ceramic squeak. "You can hardly keep him in training only to run one more lackluster race. And if you drop him in class we stand to lose him."

Well, that wasn't a possibility for one second. *No one* was ever going to put a claim tag on that horse's halter. We'd worked too hard to find him. He was *ours*—end of story. Alexander knew that as well as I did. He was just mouthing empty threats now. "He'll *never* go in a claiming race," I said pointlessly, simply for the sake of saying the words aloud, making sure they were still true.

"Well, there you have it. He isn't an allowance horse anymore," Alexander went on dourly. "And there's nowhere else for him to go. If he can't win in Tampa—"

"I know." Then he couldn't win anywhere—not anywhere in Florida, anyway. Not anywhere legal and sanctioned by the state. Gulfstream Park, with its richer purses and tougher competition, was beyond his reach now.

"We'll take him home and turn him out for a little while. Then you can call Lucy Knapp and ask her to take him into training once he gets bored. She can hang on to him for six months, see what kind of career he might have ahead of him, or you can take him back for a pony. Come on, Alex. It's for the best. I don't want to see him go either, but I don't know where we'd put him. And you want to see him working, don't you? You don't want to see him fat and wasted in a pasture."

"Of course." I tried to think of excuses. "We have a big farm, though, we ought to be able to find somewhere to stick one little gelding."

"Well, we can, for a little while, anyway. But long-term? He can't stay in the training barn, the broodmares will beat him up, *he'll* beat up the yearlings, and he doesn't belong in the stallion barn."

I was quiet, running my finger around the rim of my own coffee mug, wondering why the stallion barn was out. It seemed like the perfect place to stick one little gelding who didn't have a job right now. There were four empty stalls up there, just gathering cobwebs, growing dank and moldy, wasted space we hardly noticed in a barn I rarely went near.

But Alexander held the stallion barn, and our two stallions, firmly under his own power. If he said that Tiger wasn't welcome up there, that was the end of it.

Now Alexander took a breath and made his proclamation, fingers laced together, the image of a reasonable man, a good husband, a sensible horse trainer. "Lucy can bring him along as a riding horse. We'll keep close tabs on him. We'll visit him and make sure he's happy. Once she's finished with him, we can decided the next step. If you want to keep him to ride, you can board him with her. Or we can find someone close by who can ride him, and lease him out."

I rubbed at my forehead. This wasn't supposed to happen. A barn without Tiger—I didn't want it, didn't even want to *think* about it. I'd given up Luna, I'd given up Personal Best— I saw them on trips south to check on their works, and run them in races, but that wasn't the same as having them in the barn. Now my Tiger had to go? "I never thought we'd let him go," I said reproachfully. "I thought you felt the same."

"Of course we won't let him go. I know he is our pet, and obviously we would never sell him. But he needs a job, and we'll be all right without him. There's hardly a lack of horses in the barn." Alexander's voice was gentle and reasonable, which for some reason made everything seem all the more upsetting. "You've barely gotten to know the new two-year-olds. There's bound to be a new pet in the bunch. You find one every year. Last year it was Personal Best, remember?"

"And now he's in Miami," I sniffed. "And so is Luna. That's not helpful. If I lose my favorite every year, I'm just going to stop getting attached."

Alexander shook his head, looking amused. "Oh, Alex, if only. But you'll get attached to someone new. It's in your nature. And then you can cry about him next year, too. It's your way. It's emotionally exhausting, yes, but it's just the way you are." He held up his hands and smiled as if there was nothing he could do about me, despite all his best efforts. I was unfixable.

"They're *all* dull this year," I sniffed, ignoring his teasing. "I don't know what we did wrong, or if there was something in the water or what, but not one of these babies has the personality of a banana."

Alexander gravely considered the potential personality of a banana. "Well," he said finally. "At least they'll be easy."

He had a point. Personality usually meant brains, and brains usually meant trouble. Young horses who thought too much got ideas in their heads that were not easily removed, ideas about who was in charge, the rider or the horse. Tiger was an excellent example of this. Tiger asked himself, and me, this question every single morning.

I sipped at my coffee, which had taken on the approximate taste and consistency of a truck-stop latte, and leaned back in the chair. I could see my reflection in the mirror tilted against the wall behind Alexander, resting crookedly on the dusty filing cabinet. I frowned at myself. I was thin this winter, from constant riding and farm work, and my shoulder-length blonde hair was in an untidy pony-tail that seemed to accentuate my cheekbones and chin. It wasn't really flattering. Alexander told me to eat more. But I'd been anxious constantly since the string of horses had gone to south Florida, and all I'd wanted to do was work. I'd even gone back to galloping a few horses every morning, instead of watching the sets go by from the back of a pony. When I was galloping, I wasn't thinking about anything but that horse, in that moment. It was a relief to let everything else slip away for a few minutes, and just concentrate on the sound of hoofbeats rumbling and tack jingling, to communicate to the young horse how to change his leads in the turns and how to match his strides with his work-partner.

I had to admit I'd been spending an inordinate amount of time on Tiger. Tiger, the horse who lost. I'd been so excited over his last two works. What a morning glory he'd turned out to be in the end! The loss could hardly have been more painful. Forty lengths was bad enough. Forty lengths was practically in the next race, all racetrack jokes aside. Forty lengths was a sign you might consider a new career for *yourself,* never mind your horse. But when you considered who had won that race, and with what sort of horse, it got a thousand times worse.

Mary Archer had looked like the cat that got the cream, too. I could practically hear her purring as she accepted the memorial plaque that had accompanied the race. Behind her, the horse she had won with, some Nobody by No One out of Nothing Much, had looked around the winner's circle with wild eyes. As well he should have, since it was the first time the five-year-old gelding had ever seen the inside of one. That horse blew up the board and busted a few pick-six millionaires that day. Mary Archer had looked over at me, as I sponged water over my sweaty horse's poll, and gave me a squint-eyed glare, as if I were something she'd scraped from the bottom of her shoe.

So had the press.

And the horsemen around the barns. And the bettors. And basically everyone in the world.

Tiger had been the second-favorite, you see.

Today hadn't been my best day.

Then, the gossip had hit, and Miss Mary Quite Contrary had disappeared very quickly. Back to the barns, back to her truck? Amongst the clusters of horsemen repeating the unbelievable news that had just come out of south Florida, Mary was absent. Conspicuously so, it seemed to me. But maybe that was just because of our ongoing feud. Maybe it didn't mean anything at all.

"I guess I just didn't want to believe he was so done. I knew he was slowing down, but I didn't know it would be so terrible."

"It was terrible," Alexander agreed promptly. "It was an embarrassment. It was a kick in the balls. But that's racing. It's nothing personal—he just let you know he was done, in the most public way possible." He picked up his coffee, took a sip, then quickly put down his cup as if he'd suddenly had a revelation. "Is this just about Tiger, or are you upset about Mary Archer beating you?"

I slumped in my chair. *Caught.* "A little," I admitted. "But look at the streak she's on, and with all these horses right off the claim. She's jumping them in class and they're all winning and no one is questioning that even a little bit? All this and she's training for *Littlefield,* Alexander! Horses no one else in town would touch with a ten-foot pole. That horse that beat Tiger hadn't even run at that level before, let alone put his nose in front. That's not a little nuts? And she was nowhere to be seen once the word broke about those abandoned horses. I don't know how many bad schemes one person can be in on, but I've only seen her in the worst of company, and you know it." The bush track at Otter Creek came to mind. Mary didn't worry much about social conventions, or which side of pari-mutuel law she was on.

Alexander looked around to see if anyone was listening. "Maybe this isn't a public conversation," he suggested in a reproving tone.

"Fine." He was probably right. At the races, you never knew when you were alone and when there was someone just outside the door, loitering and listening. Secrets were worth good money here.

"But whether her horses are legitimate or not, Tiger didn't get beat by a nose. He got beat by forty lengths. That's got nothing to do with the winner."

I sighed. I knew that. I *did*. But it didn't make things any better. I was still losing a horse, and I'd still seen him get beat by the woman who had tried her best to make me look like an idiot in Saratoga, and followed that up by being my only rival for a classless claimer who needed a safe retirement. I'd done all right at Saratoga despite her, and Christmasfordee would soon be safely installed in Lucy Knapp's training barn, where she would learn to be a sport-horse, but Mary was always back for more, a thorn in my side, pointing out my every mistake.

"I guess that's it then." I brushed at my tingling eyes. "This dusty barn!"

Alexander took my hand and rubbed his thumb against my palm. "We get so attached," he teased. "We really are awful at this business."

I had to smile at that, and at Alexander, and at us, two trainers with horses running and winning all over Florida, a breeding and training farm recognized the world over, and the softest damn hearts in the game. "At least we don't have a guilty conscience keeping us up at night," I said lightly. "Not everyone in this business can say that. Sure, we get our feelings hurt, but our horses are healthy and safe and happy."

Alexander nodded. "You're right about that, love." He reached across the desk and took my hand. His calloused grip was soft on mine, but I could feel the power there, the sinews and tendons and muscles and hard bone beneath leathery warm flesh. We were strong, I thought. We were mighty, and we would not let a little thing like retiring a horse bring us down. We'd provide for Tiger as we had provided for every other horse who had been entrusted to our care. We were the good guys, and even if I'd been a dismal failure as a trainer today, my day would come. Simple karma said so—karma and hard, hard work.

Alexander's phone suddenly buzzed, bouncing across the desk like an angry bee, and we both jumped. He let go of my hand to pick up the phone, and I put it back into my lap, feeling anxious, even a little cold, without his comforting touch.

Goodness, I was just all kinds of a girl tonight, wasn't I. Time to toughen up and remember who I was. I smiled at Alexander as I got up and headed back into the shed-row to find something to do. There was always something to be done. That might be the best thing about working with horses.

Find Turning for Home in ebook or paperback from your favorite bookseller.

About the Author

Like many of my characters, I live in Florida, where I write fiction and freelance for a variety of publications. In the past I've worked professionally in many aspects of the equestrian world, including grooming for top event riders, training off-track Thoroughbreds, galloping racehorses, patrolling Central Park on horseback, working on breeding farms, and more! I use all of this experience to inform the equestrian scenes in my novels. They say that truth is stranger than fiction, and those of us in the horse business will certainly agree!

Visit my website at nataliekreinert.com to keep up with the latest news and read occasional blog posts and book reviews. For previews, installments of upcoming fiction, and exclusive stories, visit my Patreon page at patreon.com/nataliekreinert and learn how you can become one of my team members.

For more, find me on social media:

- Facebook: facebook.com/nataliekellerreinert

- Group: facebook.com/groups/societyofweirdhorsegirls

- Bookbub: bookbub.com/profile/natalie-keller-reinert
- Twitter: twitter.com/nataliegallops
- Instagram: instagram.com/nataliekreinert
- Email: natalie@nataliekreinert.com